with the

Storms

catching

Dusk

with the
Storms
catching
Dusk

NELLY ALIKYAN

*To everyone who's afraid of the next step
because they've lived one version their whole life.*

ALSO BY NELLY ALIKYAN

Catchers Series

With the Flames Catching Midnight

With the Rains Catching Dawn

With the Ice Catching Twilight

With the Storms Catching Dusk

With the Winds Catching Sunlight

With the Ashes Catching Daybreak

Whittle Magic Series

Alluring Darkness

Beholding Darkness

Claiming Darkness

Desiring Darkness

ALSO BY N. ALIKYAN

Buttercup Baby

Promise of A Lifetime

CHAPTER 1

NORYA

Her back arched as his tongue slipped up her spine, ending with a bite to her shoulder.

He'd taken a tube of lube from the Remedies Expert and had two fingers slick with the gooey stuff as they entered her ass, curling to hit the perfect spot as his cock thrust into her.

Tristan was rough as he pounded into her, guttural in the sounds he made. They made no attempts to quiet themselves. They were in the Northern palace where the walls were thicker and in a room far enough away from civilization to care.

And she was an Islander. She surely didn't care if they were heard.

Norya gripped the comforter of the bed they were on as her climax hit, and she screamed, voice cracking as Tristan laughed behind her.

"That's three, little warrior," he teased. "I think you bet I couldn't make you come nine times before I came once?"

His fingers rubbed over her clit so ferociously, Norya's eyes rolled back, and she bit into the comforter, his other hand still fucking her ass. She wanted to fight her orgasm so he wouldn't have the satisfaction of winning this bet, but as his cock pounded into her, she couldn't fight it. Tristan's dick slipped out as she squirted all over the sheets, the liquid coming out of her in puddles before he was able to put his cock back in her.

"That's a good fucking girl," he ground out as the door opened to the room, and both of them turned to find the Princess of the Northern Lands standing there with a look of shocked fright.

By the sounds of her screams, Rosaelia had probably thought her in danger and come for some aid. The crimson of her cheeks said she now realized how very mistaken she'd been.

Sael muttered an apology and slammed the door shut behind her.

It made both Tristan and Norya laugh as he flipped her onto her back. Tristan leaned down to kiss her as they shared this moment laughing at the Princess.

"My poor Princess has quite the habit," he teased.

"Your poor Princess may be traumatized."

He scoffed. "Please. She fucks your brother."

She bit his bottom lip. "Very true, spy. Now, are you done? Only four?"

He gripped both of her ankles and brought them up beside her face, spreading her wide. "Not even close. Now hold your ankles."

She smirked. "I'm not helping you win."

His fingers scraped down her calves as he gave her a teasing grin, and slithered down her body, holding her legs open as he took her soaking clit into his mouth.

Norya's hands fell into his hair and she pulled at it, lost in the talented daze his tongue had the power to put her in.

Tristan pushed her legs even more so her ass lifted off the

bed, and he slipped lower to lick her puckered hole. He ate her ass as he dropped one of her legs to play with her pussy, fucking her, then rubbing her clit, then fucking her again.

It was so fucking good, Norya didn't care if he won. She held on to her ankles to keep herself open for him. Tristan only laughed at her defeat as he now had both hands free to fuck her and tease her as he ate her ass.

She came hard, squirting onto his face as he licked up her slit to suck at her clit again, to get any taste of her.

He bit the inside of her thigh. "Five."

He licked back up her body, and while she kept her legs spread by the ankles, he collared her and held her down, grinning at her from above while his face dripped with her arousal. "You ready to give up yet?"

She smirked, needing him to continue. "You're not going to win, spy. You still have halfway to go, and there's no way your cock won't explode before then."

Lies. She knew how amazing his stamina was, but she needed him riled up with the need to prove himself so he'd be rough with her the way she wanted.

His hands tightened around her neck as he lowered to kiss her. She tasted herself on his face, his tongue, every inch of him, and damn near came again. He laughed like he knew what he did to her.

Then he peeled away and got off the bed.

Just like that.

She growled. "Spy! Get your ass back over here!"

He laughed again as he stood to the side of the bed and reached over to take a fistful of her hair. He dragged her toward himself so her head fell over the edge, and his hands teased her mouth. "Open that mouth, little whore."

She was overjoyed at the prospect of getting his cock in her mouth as he tapped it over her lips, then slipped it into her waiting mouth. She moaned at the taste of herself on his cock as his hands slid down her body, one taking a breast while the other slipped down until he had three fingers inside her.

"Suck, little warrior whore."

She laughed as drool slipped out of her mouth, but she did as she was told. Maybe she could get him to come before he hit six.

He didn't fuck her mouth like she wanted, merely stood there and let her suck him off while his fingers pounded into her, so wet with her arousal, the room sounded like a whirlpool storm was amid them.

Then he leaned down to suck and bite at her nipples.

She didn't want to come. Didn't want to give him that satisfaction.

But with his mouth on her nipples, his fingers in her pussy, and his cock shoved down her throat, there was no stopping it. She came, spraying all over while her moans gagged on his cock.

He didn't stop fucking her pussy until her orgasm—which lasted an eternity—ended.

Then he quickly pulled his cock from her mouth with a loud groan.

"No!" she fought, reaching for his dick again.

He grabbed both of her wrists and forced them away. "No, no, darling. We're only at six."

"Cheater!" she yelled.

He collared her to force her up to her knees, her withered body barely able to do as he wanted. "I never said I wouldn't cheat, little barbarianette."

She growled and bit his bottom lip, making it bleed.

"Give me three more little orgasms, then you can tell me whether you want my cum in your mouth, your pussy, or your ass."

"What if I want it on me?"

"Not an option tonight," he growled as he bit her shoulder.

She laughed at his sounds, knowing he wanted to come desperately, and started pumping his cock.

He pushed her hands away, and forced her onto all fours. "No touching me, whore."

She shoved her ass back. "You're no fun, Northerner."

He bit, kissed, and licked at her ass as he reached for the tube of lube once more, drenching his cock and fingers with it. His soaked fingers reached for her puckered hole, playing with and teasing it. "I think you talk too much, Islander."

He placed his cock at her ass and impaled her before she could respond, making her scream out. Her eyes rolled back as he pulled on her hair to keep her upright, his other hand moving for her clit. He knew how much she loved him in her ass, and she knew he would hardly be able to last while in there.

As he stuck his fingers in her pussy, she came again.

"Seven." He laughed through his grunts.

He pulled his cock out and dropped to his knees, sucking on her clit for only a few seconds before she was squirting again.

"Eight," he teased.

"You're not gonna win," she argued, barely able to get the word out.

He sucked her clit again before rising to his feet and sticking his cock in her ass again. "You're gonna come again, whore. You know you want me to win."

He fucked her ass hard, one hand fucking her pussy while the other pinched at her clit.

He was gonna win.

He was gonna win.

She couldn't let him win.

But she needed to come.

She needed—

Needed—

"Where do you want it? Mouth, pussy, or ass?"

She couldn't let him win.

Couldn't—

Couldn't...

"Answer me!" he growled.

The sheer power in his voice, paired with what he was doing to her, had her screaming with number nine.

She was still in the middle of the orgasm when he growled, "Answer me!"

"Mouth," she cried. "I want you in my mouth!"

He pulled out of her quickly, turning her so she sat on the bed before him, and shoved his cock into her mouth. He only pumped once before he came inside her mouth, cum dripping down her chin as he continued to fill her.

His groans had her hands moving for her pussy, and orgasm ten hit her as she sucked the cum out of his cock.

When he finally pulled away, his cum was still dripping from her lips and falling onto her chest. He smirked and rubbed it into her skin as he breathed hard above her.

Norya just looked up at him in a daze.

After a few minutes to catch his breath, Tristan forced her jaw into his hand and turned her to look at the bed. "Look at the mess you made, Norya darling."

CHAPTER 2
TRISTAN

There was a mix of amused smirks and forced frowns that greeted Tristan as he walked into the top room of the palace—the one Sparrow had been in the first time the Master Magician had been on palace grounds, standing only a few yards from Tristan and the Princess.

He knew what the looks were about.

He wanted to be ashamed. His Northern blood was ashamed, but realistically, he could never help but find it funny.

"Men," he opened as he took the seat between Miels and Killian, the latter only there as a show of trying to bond with them as it was obvious he would rather be with the hunters. The man was married to the Princess of the Northern Lands, making him the future King, so he really had no choice, but he didn't hide his disapproval.

With Sparrow beside Miels and James on Killian's other side, these meetings were the best way for Killian to bond with the four of them as it also included learning information that could keep his princess—the nation's Princess—safe.

"Ro was *red* when she found us out on the greens," Miels teased as an opening.

Tristan's grin grew. "I cannot blame her this time. Nor was quite loud, and I can see how it may have been misinterpreted." He turned to Killian. "But you really should have a talk with your woman. I think she enjoys watching duos. Maybe your barbarian cum is starting to affect her."

Even though the Islander didn't like them, Tristan had become comfortable around the man. And with no women about, he was at ease to use language he kept reserved for his closest males.

"Or maybe you lot sheltered her too much," Killian argued. "I had nothing to do with how dirty my girl's fantasies are." He smirked. "I only make them realities for her."

"Okay," Sparrow started before any of them could say any more about Rosaelia's sex life. "That's enough about our sister." He glared at Tristan as he said those final words.

Tristan picked at the papers they had scattered around the round table. "What are you lot going over? And where's Ed?"

Miels shrugged. "He said he needed to go down to the tailor's, but I saw Odolf in the kitchens, and apparently they didn't have a meeting, so I don't know. Maybe he wanted away from us for a day. Poor man deals with too much."

"You lot going off about his daughter's sex life doesn't help," Sparrow argued.

Tristan smirked in his direction. "But you degrading his other daughter with all the filthy things you two do does?"

Sparrow's grin was wicked as a response. "He's never seen Evony as a daughter. He's simply happy I keep her in check."

Tristan met James's, then Miels's shining eyes as they all hummed their disbelief, but it was Killian, the member here not yet comfortable with all the teasing, that brought them back to the matters of importance. "We were discussing this plague—the Oriion, it's been decided—that seems to be getting more prominent. It wasn't brought on by the Island, but it's getting more widespread in the northern parts of these lands."

Tristan's humor vanished. They'd been hoping it was a normal flu like any other, one that would pass with time. It happened every couple of years, a new virus that made the population ill but was gone almost as quickly as it came. It was the only reason they'd waited this long to truly do anything about it. "Yes, I've noticed. And with the Master Sorcerer gone, healing them will be a nightmare."

"Maybe not," Sparrow muttered in thought, his gaze long gone.

"Do you know something?" James asked.

Sparrow brought himself back from his thoughts. "Etel is obviously as helpful as she can be, but as one person, and not a Master at that, she can only do so much as the Remedies Expert. But I think I know someone who might be able to heal this. If we can figure out what it is."

They all sat up straighter.

"Who?" Killian asked in that harsh tone of his.

Sparrow eyed him for a long time before turning to meet Tristan and Miels's gazes. "Have you suspected her at all? Of being the Master Healer?"

Tristan met his identical mate's gaze. Only one person could possibly come close to holding that title.

It had been something to cross his mind a time or two, but he'd never focused on the matter.

"Ashtyn?" Killian asked.

"What makes you think so?" Sparrow questioned.

"She's the one who came with you to the Island. If there was anyone to bring to the Island, it would be a Master."

Sparrow's brown orbs turned to them again, and finally,

Miels answered, "I've considered it, but I figured she must not be if…"

"If she hasn't been named," Tristan finished.

Sparrow nodded. "Evony thought the same thing, but we all know naming Masters doesn't come without its faults. If they hadn't heard of her, if she didn't make herself known, then they wouldn't have known to name her."

They all considered that. Not much was known of Ashtyn's past, which really spoke to how private a life she had. So private, it wasn't unthinkable to not have heard of her down in the Southern Lands where Masters were named.

Miels leaned forward. "What does she think about being named the Master?"

"She doesn't like it, but if she ends up helping all those people up north, there's no way she won't be found out. And there's no way she won't help them, it's her calling," Sparrow answered.

"So our job now is to find out what exactly is causing this plague before we find out if we're possibly going to out Ash as a Master?" Tristan clarified.

Sparrow nodded, eyes darkening in thought once again.

Miels huffed and leaned back in his chair. "Until then, you said it yourself—Etel is our best bet. She wanted to run something past you—though I told her she didn't need your permission, as part of the Posse, she can do little things like these."

Sparrow smirked. "Give the girl time. She'll get used to being part of us eventually."

Tristan scoffed. "You just like that she honors you the way we won't."

Sparrow winked, then turned to Miels. "What is it?"

"She wants to call on apothecaries from the regions up north, teach them some things that might help their towns and villages. She thinks if they know more, then they'll be of more use. She's just been a little nervous since she's only begun teaching Gemma a few months ago, and she's still tweaking the way she does it."

Sparrow's eyes shined. "That's an extraordinary idea. Why would she ever question whether we would want that done?"

Miels smirked. "Like you said, my little creature is still learning her own capabilities."

Tristan smirked. "Your little creature has you by the balls."

It wasn't often that Tristan trained the guards. Normally, he was more the communications liaison between the palace and the public. He was good at changing the way he spoke depending on who he was with—it was why everyone thought him so reserved, but in reality, he was sort of a pig.

But the others had wives and other matters to look into, so Tristan had taken on the responsibility.

He only made half of his training physical. The other half put the guards into groups of four or five so they could practice their communications as well. Tristan wouldn't always be around to do the talking, and he needed everyone to feel comfortable doing so.

Tristan spent most of that time moving from group to group to hear how they were doing and to give pointers. Some of the men were naturals, like Tristan, so he placed them with those who were having a harder time with it.

It gave him moments in the time he moved from one group to another to think about how his life had turned out. He'd been an orphan when he'd found Miels—another orphan but one who looked exactly like Tristan. They'd thought it the perfect plan to pretend to be twins and gather what was needed to survive. Sometimes that meant being the cute twin boys who pulled on the heartstrings of older couples, especially women. Sometimes it meant using one of them to distract while the other snuck into the back of a store in order to get enough food for the week.

They'd only been at it for about six weeks when King Edmund of the Northern Lands found them. They hadn't known the man was out in the night, watching the moon as he leaned against the inn's building when they'd approached an older couple. Miels, ever the charmer, had been the distraction. Tristan's job was to sneak around them to the picnic basket they had with them and steal the entire thing. It wasn't something they were very proud of, so they tried to only take from those wealthier, but they were kids with the need for survival so they did what had to be done.

Tristan had run off with the basket into the dark corners surrounding the inn, Miels following behind only a few seconds after. They'd been giddy, holding the basket between them because there had to be enough food in there for most of the week. And now they had a basket they could hold their findings in.

What they hadn't been expecting was to bump into someone in the dark of the night. And especially not the King of the lands, one who had been introduced to the town farther northeast to the palace earlier that morning.

They'd both been wide-eyed and ready to bolt when Edmund's hand on either of their shoulders had stopped them. There'd been a gleam in his eyes and a wide smile about his lips. "Boys, boys, boys."

Their clothes, though cleaned in the rivers every other day, weren't in the best shape—Edmund said that's what truly gave away their stations. That they weren't stealing simply to steal; that they weren't merely street kids taking to survive, but they were young boys who wanted a certain lifestyle and stealing was simply done to keep them strong enough to reach for it.

Nonetheless, he and Miels had been terrified to be caught by the King. But then the man took the basket from them and left it just out of the darkened area for the couple to find—and think it was a trick for jest—and took them to his suite where he gave them access to a true bath, a hot meal, and new clothes. They spent the night telling the King about their lives and had been part of the family since.

And since, both he and Miels—and Sparrow—did whatever they could to be by the King's side. He'd just been entering his later twenties—the same age Tristan was now—and was a single father to a Princess with no responsibilities to the three of them, but he'd taken them in any way. They'd been lucky. Out of all the children in the Northern Lands, they were the ones he'd been drawn to.

He'd never treated them differently either. They'd always been part of the family. It was part of the reason Sparrow had been willing to allow Edmund to question Evony when they thought she was the rebel leader. The King had always been loyal to them, so they did whatever they could to make sure they were worth it. Not because Edmund expected it, but because they wanted to.

In fact, Edmund did exactly the opposite of expecting anything from them. He truly thought of them as his sons and wanted to give them the life any of his children would get. It was why there was always guilt in his eyes when he was around Evony. Even though it was still difficult to entirely see her as his daughter, she was, and she'd been stripped of the opportunity to grow up as such. Tristan knew it ate away at the King.

He brought himself back to the training the guards were going through. He was standing before a group of five as one of them practiced being the liaison. He pretended all four of his friends were common folk and needed to be convinced that everything would be all right and the King was always looking out for them. He was one of the best and definitely one Tristan would use in the future when he needed aid.

Tristan moved silently to the next group, his gaze catching onto the changing of the leaves outdoors. A small smile graced his lips at the sight. It had been nearing autumn when he and Miels had been found, and oh, what a different life they lived now.

CHAPTER 3
TRISTAN

Tristan never spent much time with the hunters, but Norya had pulled on his competitive streak, so he was out with them after his work with the guards was over.

It wasn't a surprise that both Islanders had joined the hunters rather than any of the other groups in the palace. As barbarians who had to fend for themselves, feed themselves and their family, they'd grown up great hunters. They were proving quite valuable to the palace's feedings.

And though Norya and Killian had joined the group almost immediately upon coming to the palace, Tristan never particularly cared to see them at work.

But now, Norya was teasing him about his abilities, and he couldn't have that. He would show her that though she may be an extraordinary huntress because of her lifetime—which included a whole year over Tristan's own twenty-seven—of training, he was going to be just as good on his first try.

Did he truly believe any of that? No.

Was he going to let Norya know he didn't believe any of it? Abso-fucking-lutely not.

And if, along the way, he happened to beat her, Tristan already had plans for all the ways he'd delight in her losing their competition.

They moved into the forest with the other hunters, but it didn't take long for Norya to pull on his arm with that devious smirk across her features. The others would think they were scurrying away to fuck.

It made the hairs on the back of his neck stand—others thinking he was doing that out in the open—because of his Northern upbringing, but Tristan couldn't blame them. At this point, he and Norya had been caught at least a couple dozen times. Though it was well-known that though the Posse didn't have fuck buddies within the palace, he and Norya were an exception for one another. His Northern blood hated being caught. He didn't want the world to see the cheeky—and devious—side he showed the Posse, needed to remain poised and serious around the others.

But when Norya was around him, he couldn't help himself. He had a need, like a fiend, to touch and taste her. To be touched and tasted by her.

Norya walked them until they were in a clearing a little ways from the others, then turned to him. "Do you know how to use your weapon, little spy?" She gave a little pout with the question as if she were speaking with a child and needed to be kind.

Tristan ground his jaw to hide his amusement—and suppress his need to turn her around and turn her ass red—and rolled his eyes. "I can shoot an arrow, little warrior."

"Good." She turned with a smile on her face. "One kill each. Let's see who loses."

Norya shot at a squirrel lazily walking along a branch, and

she looked like a goddess doing so. She was built and stronger than half the men at the palace, her hair was almost always braided back, and she gave most Northerners a look that could be passed off as cold and uninviting. Tristan's cock turned hard for all of it.

It turned extra hard witnessing her extraordinary talent in the forests.

She lowered her bow and arrow but didn't turn to him. Her voice was smug as she said, "Your turn."

Tristan ignored the weapon at his back and threw his dagger like this was one of the dagger trainings he did with his brothers. It hit a squirrel that could hardly be seen straight in the chest.

Norya turned on him. "Cheater!"

"Where is it written that hunting must be done with an arrow? I seem to remember your brother does all of his with a dagger."

Norya huffed with a scowl as she moved to take her kill. "You still cheated."

Tristan laughed as he followed, taking his dagger from his own kill, and wiping the blood on his pant leg. "I don't think so."

They walked only another few yards before Norya stopped them and dropped her kill, Tristan following in her heed. She nodded toward a bush, and Tristan saw it—a family of rabbits, though there didn't seem to be any babies among them.

"We'll have to hit together otherwise they'll go scurrying and we won't both get a chance," she whispered so as not to alert them of their presence.

Tristan nodded, readying his dagger. "Whatever you say, my little huntress."

She raised her own weapons. "I'm not your little anything, spy."

Tristan's lips twitched up as they both readied, then released their weapons, Norya's arrow and his dagger landing perfectly into two rabbits.

As they moved for the animals, he said, "That's not true, Nor." As they added the squirrels to the rabbit pile, and Norya met his gaze once more, he smirked. "You're my little whore."

She rolled her eyes but couldn't fight her annoyed grin. "Hopefully we can attract something bigger now."

Tristan leaned back into a tree. "You wanna fuck while we wait?"

She gave him a once over. "As tempting as your plans are," she said in the most baritone, bored voice conceivable. "We'll be too distracted if we're fucking to get a kill in. Or worse, we'll be so distracted the beast will attack us instead."

Tristan knew as much. "You're no fun."

She shrugged. "Beat me, and I'll suck your dick."

He snorted. "When I beat you, you're doing far more than just sucking my dick, Nor."

"And when I beat you?"

"I'll eat your pussy until you pass out? You think I can kill you from all the pleasure?"

She eyed him like she was hungry. "So I win, and my prize is you kill me?"

He threw his arm over her shoulders and pulled her into his side for a kiss on the crown. "With pleasure."

She chuckled, then hushed him as the huntress in her picked up a threat coming for them. Not a second later, the eyes of a beast slowly prowling for the kills left in the clearing was noticeable behind the trees.

"You first." She pushed him away.

Tristan lifted his bow and arrow this time and aimed for the thing. He wasn't so great with this weapon, but he was carrying it so might as well use it.

When he released his arrow, the thing went flying straight for the beast's leg, but it wasn't a kill shot. The beast turned wild eyes around, and when he couldn't find the source of the wound, he whimpered back slowly. His wide eyes searched the area before he turned down to pull the arrow from his leg, readying himself to flee.

Norya snorted. "Splendid job."

Tristan didn't actually care about not killing the thing, but as he turned for Norya, preparing for her shot, he realized that he couldn't allow her to win. Not only because of the things he'd like to do to her when he won but because he couldn't allow her to have that satisfaction.

Norya smirked at him as her arms raised with the bow and arrow aimed at the beast. She was going to get it perfectly between the eyes and show Tristan that she was superior.

He couldn't have that.

His hand slipped over her ass and between her legs until he was cupping her pussy from behind.

Her breath hitched. "Get your hands off me, fucker."

He rolled his fingers. "I thought you were an extraordinary hunter. Kill it, little whore."

She grumbled curses at him as she steadied her breathing and focused her aim once more. Tristan waited until her fingers were beginning to slip from the arrow before he pressed into her clit and had her entire body flinching with desire.

The arrow hit the ground three feet from the beast and had the thing running—stumbling with his wounded leg—off in fear as Norya turned on him. "Fucking cheater!"

His fingers still played at her pussy as he leaned in. "I don't remember there being any clauses when you said you could hit anything, anytime. They were your words, little barbarianette. I was simply checking if they were true."

She moved so quickly, Tristan hardly processed it before

she had his hand off her and her weapons raised toward him, the arrow staring his nose straight down. "Any*thing*, cheater."

Tristan stepped closer so the pointed edge of the arrow spiked into his nose. "You know you would never hurt me. Who else is supposed to spank that ass raw or fill that mouth when it talks too much shit?"

"There're plenty of men here." She smirked.

"Yet you keep bringing that pussy to my suite and sitting on my face."

Norya looked like she was about to release the arrow simply to prove a point when a cry was heard from one of the others killing the beast that had run off, then Killian appeared as he growled from the other side of the clearing, "Will you two stop fucking around and hunt."

Norya swiped her weapons away, scraping Tristan's nose in the process to leave a small cut, as she grumbled beneath her breath, "Conceited *little* fucker."

Tristan laughed as he followed her. "You've had my cock in all of your holes. I think you're well aware it's quite large."

"Next time you come, I'm turning your cock, so you give yourself a facial."

Tristan laughed. "As long as you lick it off my face, my whore."

She turned with a sinister glimmer in her eyes as her hips swayed. Her smirk told him she delighted in his words, and Tristan had a feeling she was truly going to do the things she threatened. He couldn't say he minded.

CHAPTER 4
NORYA

The nonas spent so much time with Etel, the Remedies Expert and Miels's wife, that Norya never had to think too hard about it before she decided to check for them there.

And she found them almost every single time.

When they'd learned that Etel gave her remedies lessons to Gemma, the Master Magician's best friend, they'd jumped at the idea of having their own lessons. Now they were helping the girl prepare so when she began teaching apothecary owners, the lessons would run smoothly.

"Ah, look who has graced us with her presence." Nona Tereza gave her a sneaky grin.

Norya rolled her eyes. "We share a suite, Nona. I see you every day."

"Yes, but you make it sound like such a task. You see us because we live in the same quarters, but not so often during the day. And look at poor little Etel"—she played with the expert's hair—"how do you think she feels when you never come to see her."

"Oh, stop it, Nona." Norya sat on a stool to watch them.

Nona Tereza laughed. "Okay. So why don't you tell me why you're here?"

Norya shrugged. "I missed Eleni."

"Ha. Ha. Very funny, deary."

"I don't know. I heard Etel's preparing to teach the apothecary owners, and I wanted to hear her thoughts as a remedy maker about what she thinks could be behind this plague up north, especially because it's concentrated to the northern parts of the Northern Lands only, no other parts of these lands and not so far up as the Island."

"What makes you think I would know?" Etel asked.

"Nothing. I just figure there's something in you that understands nature better than any of the rest of us. Could it possibly be something related to that rather than an illness that someone caught and passed on?"

She paused. "I hadn't thought of that per se. I'm sure the boys have though. If that were the case, I suspect they would've checked for it already."

"There was a tree about ten years ago on the Island. We didn't know it was dying, so we didn't cut it down. It ended up infesting the fields around it. By the time we figured out it was because of the tree and not simply someone sabotaging—the sorcerers helped with that—then we could truly take care of it. I just think you might know how things are supposed to be since you use them in order to make your remedies."

Etel smiled like she was glad Norya saw the talent in her, though it'd be difficult not to. "I will talk to Miels. I'm sure they've already looked into it, but I'll see. But off the top of my head, I cannot think of anything to tell you. It will be something that I see, hear, feel that will alert me to the trouble. I may be able to think of some more obvious signs now, but those are things that anyone would notice. For the more hidden ones, I don't think I'd be able to think of it unless I was there."

"Then I will not fight for you to travel with us for your expertise until we decide it must be by nature."

Etel smiled as Nona Tereza said, "I don't think it is. It is infesting the humans, not the plantation around them. I think this is by someone's doing. Or a cold that has blown up."

"That's what I'm afraid of too," Norya conceded. "Especially considering only earlier this year you had that rebellion brewing and the attack on the palace. Who's to say something in that nature isn't the reason behind this as well. Rowena might be dead, but we couldn't get to all of her allies. We don't even know of all of her allies."

"I'll take extra thought about it," Etel said. "I'll make a list of the more obvious things I think it can be and make sure to teach the apothecary owners something for each of those on top of what I already had planned. Thank you, Norya."

"Do not thank me. This is where I live now, and I would much rather not have that plague travel down here and infect me as well."

Nona Tereza smirked. "Or affect Tristan."

Norya returned the devious look. "We cannot have anything tampering with his stamina, now, can we?"

"Is that the only reason?" Her eyes twinkled.

Norya rolled her eyes. Nona Tereza was like a hound after a bloody meal. Once she held on to an idea, she didn't let go. She'd been the same when Killian met Sael. And though that had turned out favorable, it had also been a case in which Killian wanted to claim a woman. Norya didn't want to be claimed. It was never something she'd dreamed of.

"We've been fucking for three months, Nona. I think if I was going to fall for him, I would've done so already."

"Who's to say you haven't?" she teased.

"Yet you wonder why I do not wish to spend more of my days with you. Poor Nona Eleni misses out on my company because of your ploys."

"What ploys?" She shrugged, making herself look innocent.

"The Island turned that Northern blood in you black. You're too devious to be from here."

Nona Tereza laughed. "Oh hush and come help us bag these herbs. We need to have them ready for when the apothecary owners come."

Norya smiled and moved to help them, standing beside Nona Tereza, and giving her a hip bump. She loved the nonas for this reason specifically—they teased her, made her feel like family. Even Nona Eleni, who hardly spoke, said much with the way she'd look at Norya.

She took a small pouch and began filling it with lavender while Nona Tereza worked on filling another pouch with thyme. Nona Eleni worked on peeling the herbs off the stems while they all spoke to Etel about which lessons she should teach—in which order, how long she may need to spend on each. It helped to have Norya there as someone unfamiliar with the process to truly understand that some lessons may need to be slowed down.

The entire day made Norya happy in a way similar to hunting, except this was something she could do with her family.

THERE WERE no large libraries on the Island.

At least, none that Norya had ever been to. The closest she ever came was the bookshops, and they were never as large as the North's palace library.

This was a behemoth of a space with two stories—the top one looking over the bottom—and a nice sanctuary from the rest of the world.

Though Norya wasn't much of a reader of fiction, she'd pulled out two books on sewing to take a look at. She knew she could simply go to the tailors and ask for help, but she didn't want to distract them from their jobs.

Sat on the top floor with her legs falling through the railings to dangle in the air, Norya had one sewing book laid open atop another as she tried to thread the needle she'd taken from the tailor's wing with a string. She had an insurmountable amount of patience because of the life of hunting and fending for herself she'd lived, so she was ready to spend as long as necessary to get this skill.

She wasn't even sure why she wanted to learn it. It was simply always something she thought she would need. Growing up, she'd wanted to learn so she could mend her own clothes and not need to rely on others, but with surviving, it had always been pushed down the list of things to do.

Now she had time.

So as her legs dangled, she pulled the piece of cloth she'd taken for practice and tried to follow the instructions in the book on how to simply thread the needle through the cloth and out the other side.

It took her concentration in order not to prick herself which was possibly the reason Norya had decided to finally start learning. She needed this. On the Island, she had the distraction of always needing to be alert to survive, but it was much more relaxed in the Northern Lands, and especially at the palace. She was still alert, a lifetime wouldn't be pushed aside so easily, but it wasn't the same need. Now she needed something to keep her thoughts at bay.

She wanted a couple hours where she could forget that

there were parts of growing up on the Island that she would never experience again now living on the Northern Lands.

She wanted to forget that though she had the nonas and Killian still, now also had the Posse, and Tristan as a best friend, she still felt alone.

Wanted to forget that growing up with the need to survive had made it impossible for her to learn to make friends, and now she felt awkward around those within the palace. Would she ever grow connections with them? With the women specifically?

As she sewed the hem of the cloth, Norya was able to simply breathe and live in the moment. It was such a reprieve. Was this how the tailors worked? Free of mind? It was their calling, so maybe they were so accustomed to the job that they had space to think about things, but maybe not. Hunting was Norya's calling, and still, over two decades of doing so, her mind cleared when she was holding up her bow and arrow. It just wasn't as easy to get the reprieve that way any longer because any hunter might see her and wish to join.

She might have to speak with someone about sending her off alone. She missed hunting on her own.

Until then, she breathed and worked. At ease as she pricked her finger one too many times. This wasn't the most difficult of tasks, but Norya knew she had a learning curve ahead of her, and she smiled at the prospect. She loved the journey to learning new things, loved the time it took to get good at something she couldn't do.

CHAPTER 5
NORYA

The tavern Tristan brought them to was loud and atmospheric and almost reminded Norya of the Island. She was sure that's why he'd chosen this specific one, but she wouldn't tease him for it. He was a thoughtful friend.

And she was a good friend. After hearing him say he couldn't go whoring anymore since Miels was taken and it was no fun going out alone a couple of times in the past few months, Norya offered her companionship. Though she'd be lying if she said she didn't do so merely because she was curious.

They'd taken concoctions from Etel for the next morning to make sure no infections or diseases came from these people—and to make sure Norya and whatever woman Tristan picked didn't fall pregnant. Now, to find their playthings for the night.

"So how does this work? We stay together? Is that why you need companionship?"

He smirked. "No. Usually we separate."

"Then why is it more fun with a friend?"

He shrugged. "We could save each other if need be. We have our own jokes. We help each other if the friend of the one we're with might be interested. We don't need to be together the entire time, but we find moments that make it fun."

Norya narrowed her gaze. "Whatever you say."

He kneaded the back of her neck. "It'll be fun. Like when you went to the tavern with Kill and Ro the night we showed up."

Norya smiled. She'd fucked a big muscled guy that night. He'd made her come so hard she'd nearly blacked out. "Fine. Go find a whore then."

He smacked her ass as he walked away. "You too."

Norya eyed the tavern. There were a good amount of hot guys to choose from, but as she eyed the women, she realized most of them weren't built like she was. They were plumper, with soft skin and curves. Most Northerners had curves that the males loved to hold on to.

Norya didn't have any of that. She was all muscle, her ass and tits the only soft parts of her entire body.

Though she didn't question whether these guys would want to fuck, Norya couldn't see them being rough enough for her. Were any of them stronger than her to do so?

She moved through the tavern anyway, swaying her hips in that way that made her ass jiggle and Island men salivate.

It worked like a charm here too. Men were simply too easy sometimes.

She made it to the end of the tavern and turned to lean back against the wall when she caught sight of two men coming for her. She smirked. She'd had two men at once twice in her life, and while that had been fun, Norya had no plans to do so again. Which meant she had some pickings between the two. How amusing it would be to put them in competition with one another.

"Boys, boys, boys," she teased as they got close and caged her in with an arm on either side of her.

"I think you mean men, men, men," the one to her right corrected, his tone rough and sending a shock of pleasure down her body.

They were large men, muscled and less lean than Tristan. As a matter of fact, they were all muscle, and that brought comfort to Norya. Islanders tended to be bigger than Northern-ers, and a lot of the men Norya had chosen in the past were big, muscled things.

"Is that what you want?" the one to her left asked. "Three? You want us to find you another?"

She laughed, throwing her head back. She'd never had three at once, but she could picture it now—one cock in her mouth, one in her pussy, and one in her ass. Fuck, her pussy was soaking at the thought of it. "How about we see if you two even make the cut?"

Righty took her hand and slithered it down his chest until he reached his hard cock. He tightened her hold around it and growled. "I don't think you can deny this. That ass looks like it'll take it fine."

Norya was surprised a Northerner was speaking to her in such a manner, but maybe that was the point of coming to this tavern in particular. Tristan knew they were less reserved here and she would need that. The thought made her smile. He truly was always thinking of her desires.

Righty took the smile to mean something else and leaned forward with a wide grin of his own.

"That as tight as you can hold me?" She eyed the hand on her wrist. It was definitely tight for a normal Northerner, but it felt measly at best on her.

He leaned back a little, affronted by the remark, as his hold tightened. "You want it rough, sweet cheeks?" He eyed his friend. "I think she wants to be put in her place, Ralf."

Ralf chuckled as his hand slithered up Norya's body, thumb caressing her hardened nipples before he collared her. "Is that right?"

It was right, and though they thought they were doing something with the way they held her, it wasn't enough. Tristan may be leaner than the two of them, but damn, did his hands work wonders on her body that these two couldn't muster.

She eyed them both, bored. "That's it?"

Righty laughed. "Sweetheart, we'd destroy you."

She quirked a brow. "Maybe it's this third member that would destroy me because you two hardly have a grasp."

Ralf's hand tightened around her throat, and Righty's tightened around her wrist as the former gritted, "We can kill you right now, little girl."

Her lips tipped up at the insinuation.

When they growled and tried to get even rougher with her —not sexually but like they wanted to truly hurt her now— Norya stopped playing with them, and knocked both hands off her. She had both of their arms twisted back until they fell to a knee each and leaned down to whisper to both at once, "Don't try to scare me, boys. It's amusing at best."

They growled but didn't try anything else. Clearly they knew when they were defeated, and if they tried anything more, they'd prove to the entire tavern that a girl beat them. Then they'd have no fucks for the night. At least they were smart enough not to allow pride to beat them.

She pushed away and turned for the middle of the tavern where she stopped at a tall table. There was a sexy muscled man who eyed her, but by the way he was only whispering to the woman beside him—hands lightly skimming her sides—it was clear his thoughts were more Northern than brutish like she was used to.

Norya huffed and turned to scan the rest of the tavern. There was a good mix of muscled and leaner builds among the men, but Norya felt disheartened that any of them would do her needs justice.

She eyed another big one at the other end of the tavern who was eyeing her like a child with sweets, but when she smirked his way, eyes gleaming with all the visions of what they could do together, his cheeks pinked, and he turned for his cup.

Norya grimaced, falling back against the table once again as she scanned the place. Tristan was more lean than muscle and he took care of her perfectly, so maybe that's what she needed. Maybe it was the more lean men who would be able to give her a night to remember.

As she searched the area for one, her heart sank at what she saw. There were more men whispering and skimming women's curves, but not much more than that. There were men softly taking the hands of women to lead them out of the tavern for their private rendezvouses. The closest thing she saw to her likings were a few men truly fondling their women, but it didn't feel like enough.

And those men seemed to have a particular interest in the more curvy of the women, and Norya definitely didn't fit that arena.

Tristan was at the other end of the tavern, leaning on a stool with two women trying to get his attention. He smiled and flirted with both, letting them touch him, and he looked to be having a good time.

From observation, Norya couldn't believe how very Northern he was in that moment. If she were to step into this tavern on her own, Norya wasn't sure she would've chosen

Tristan. Though those eyes were captivating enough to gravitate over to him, outwardly, he didn't give the impression that he could, and would, do all the things he'd done to her.

Which made finding a Northern man impossible. How was she supposed to know what they were capable of if they didn't show it? Things were much easier in the Island where propriety was less of a concern.

Like he could feel her eyes on him, Tristan glanced her way and winked.

Norya scanned the rest of the space. Every man that her pussy might get wet for was either not meeting her eyes, which meant they weren't confident enough to handle her; barely touching the women they were next to so her Islander fucking-in-public blood wouldn't be satisfied; or had all of their attention on the curves of the Northern women.

Norya crossed her arms and turned back to Tristan. Maybe she wasn't such a good friend because she no longer wanted to be there.

She moved for him and stopped between the two girls vying for his attention. She crossed her arms before her chest and annoyingly felt a pout take place. "I don't like it here."

He gave her a pout in turn as his eyes shined. "Aw. Why not, little barbarianette?"

"They're too soft. I can manhandle them faster than they can blink."

He laughed, head thrown back and loud. Fucking sexy. Now her pussy was wet and ready.

Both women eyed Norya like they would cut her if she tried to take their man. She'd like to see them try. It would be far more entertaining than any of the men at this tavern.

"Aw." Tristan's finger played with her jaw. "Are you saying I'm the only one that fucks you, right?"

"In the North," she grumbled, though the memories of her

previous fucks were slowly dwindling away, replaced with the things this spy did to her.

He chuckled and pushed out of his seat. "Sorry, ladies. Friends come first, and my friend here isn't happy with the cocks in this place."

"We aren't either!" one shrieked.

"You're the cock we want!" the other stated.

Tristan gave her a conceited grin.

Norya rolled her eyes. "Do not spoil your night because of the uselessness of the men here. I'm going back to the inn. Have fun with them."

Because they were too far out from the palace, they'd gotten rooms at the inn across from the tavern. Maybe she could be like Sael and pass her night reading. Or maybe she'd find a sewing kit and get some practice in. Yes, that sounded more like it.

And though her night wasn't ending the way she'd hoped, she truly wished for Tristan to have fun with one or both of those women.

She'd just stepped out of the tavern when an arm landed around her shoulders and brought her close to his side. Norya eyed the familiar form. "What are you doing?"

He grinned down at her. "This is fun when it's with a friend."

She stopped walking. "Well, apparently, I can't be that friend for you, and I highly doubt you'll be able to find someone else like Miels." Though she didn't understand why he needed a friend. They were completely independent in there.

"I know, which is why I'd given up on the idea of whoring when he found Etel, and why I was glad to have a fuck buddy in you. *You* said you wanted to try this. I didn't ask for it."

"And I'm still annoyed it wasn't successful," she grumbled

low, but by the way he brought her in close to comfort, he still heard it.

"It's okay, Nor." He started walking them again. "We'll go back to the inn, and I'll fuck you just the way you want it."

"Thank you," she grumbled.

He laughed as he kissed her crown. "That's my good little whore."

She elbowed his gut but smiled nonetheless. "You're annoying."

CHAPTER 6
TRISTAN

The library was quiet, not many people frequented it often. Rosaelia was actually one of the only keepers with the amount of time she spent there. She, the servants who cleaned it, and the two librarians who kept a log of everything within it. Those two women normally spent all of their time in their offices on the top floor of the library.

Tristan couldn't blame them. The offices led straight into their suites, so they could do their work and take care of their families all at once. They were sweet women, each with a husband—one part of the hunters, and the other a guard—and two kids. Tristan's favorite parts of being in the library were the off-chance times he caught those four kids running around playing catch. It made him want to join them, made him excited for James and Sparrow's kids, for when Miels had a kid. He couldn't wait to chase around all of his nieces and nephews.

But alas, he was stuck between the shelves—never dusty because of the meticulous care of their keepers—with Miels as they finished the books they'd been searching through for months. They had a stack of notes each and were now in the process of dwindling down all the facts they'd learned into a concise reader.

Etel plopped down at the head of the table between the two of them and smiled. "Okay. Let's start organizing."

Her sweet smile made Tristan less grouchy knowing they would be stuck there all afternoon. And her work as a remedy maker may be able to eliminate a few of their notes as something she could teach the apothecary owners rather than something a Master would be needed for.

"All right. A reminder that the symptoms we've heard of as of now aren't many," Tristan started. "Problem is, they're also pretty common ones—sweating and freezing, vomiting and coughing, lack of appetite and dehydration. And one big one that just came in—the tips of their fingers are beginning to turn a deep blue. And most importantly—it's not contagious. There're people who stay and take care of them who are fine. People who have shared drinking glasses with them who are fine." That was the biggest 'what the fuck' about this whole thing. "It's why we named it the Oriion, a hunter in its truest form. Hidden and taking lives without a hint of detection." Like his little warrior off with the hunting groups at that very moment.

Etel's disheartened look was warming. She was such a sweet one, cared so much for others, that hearing about all of this made her hurt almost like she had the plague herself. "We're gonna figure this out. We have to."

Miels squeezed his wife's hand, then took the first sheet from his stack of notes, and summarized it. "The Island Massacre—dated two hundred years ago, created by sorcerers in order to dwindle down the population so to make living on the Island more comfortable and sustainable for the other citizens. Survival of the fittest. If they couldn't make it out of that sickness, they didn't deserve to live on the Island."

They'd made sure to document a summary of every plague or sickness, even the ones that didn't seem relevant, and added which book and page it was from in case they needed more information on it later.

Etel frowned. "A possibility, I suppose, considering Rowena was able to come down to the North so a sorcerer would be able to as well." She wrote 'Island Massacre, year 402' in the 'Possibility' column, then met their gazes again. "Next."

Tristan took a sheet. "The dead fish plague. Dated three hundred years ago. Too many fish were being poisoned by the materials used to catch them so all those who ate the fish grew with sickness."

Etel wrote the name and year in the 'No' column. "All the lands have since changed the materials they work with and nothing has happened since."

Miels read the second one on his paper. "Common flu. Annual. From the change in temperature. Normally doesn't take any lives."

Etel added it to the 'No' pile. "I believe we've all guessed it not that by now."

Tristan huffed. "And we need to figure this out soon. Winter is coming, and if they have this plague and common flu going around, they'll be taken faster."

"We'll figure it out." Etel gave that reassuring, soft smile. "Ashtyn will help you guys heal anyone who needs it."

"What we really need is for her to heal the source of the problem," Miels grumbled.

Etel's hand landed on his arm, rubbing soothing circles with her thumb. "She will, my big creature."

He gave her a teasing smirk, and Tristan knew they were quickly going to be swept up in one another if he didn't interrupt. "Rasacan Plague. Dated thirty-seven years ago. A plague created by a healer by the name of Albert Rasacan in order to kill a village because their taunts were part of the reason his wife threw herself off a high tree."

"A man-made plague by a healer. That's very possible." She added it to the appropriate column. "Ashtyn would then for sure be able to heal it, especially as a healer herself."

"The Azalea sickness. Dated one hundred years ago. In the South, by the town of Azalea. Children started eating some of the flowers that grow there on a dare. A few of them thought it would be funny to cut a few flowers up and add them to the meal at a large gathering the neighbors were having. Everyone fell sick since those flowers weren't edible. Only one dead."

Etel added it to the 'No' pile as Tristan started, "The South Southern Sickness. Dated three hundred years ago. Actually a plague, but I think they liked the alliteration. It took over the entire southern border of the South, only healed by a Master who expended too much energy. They never found the source, but after three years of healing those who fell sick—and those who fell sick multiple times—the healer passed from overuse."

Etel truly frowned, adding it to the column. "Bingo."

"Except we'll find the source this time, little creature," Miels reassured her. "We'll have Ashtyn heal that rather than the people, and it'll be added to the books for future generations."

Tristan put that sheet aside. "We'll pull that book out later. Next."

Miels grabbed another one. "The Plague of 333. A mass plague that affected the entire west side of the lands, from the top of the Island to the bottom of the South. It ran its course for three months, the symptoms so obvious that within a week, everyone in the west knew it was the same one. Turned out to be an infestation in the waters they were swimming in so not contagious."

Etel added it to the 'No' pile because this plague, while

centralized to the north of the North, was happening all over and definitely wasn't merely caused by swimming in the waters.

"The Whore's Account sickness. Dated fifty years ago. Two women got infected with a sickness by a man they had a three-way with. The symptoms didn't show themselves until a week later, after which they'd slept through over a dozen other men. All those people, and the ones they'd slept with, were put into a room and treated. Hasn't been seen since, so they got all of it."

That particular sickness Tristan had more recently found, which made him think back to his whoring past. He was extra glad after reading it that he had Etel to give him concoctions for that type of thing now, and Norya to ensure he could fuck his brains out and not have to worry about problems.

Etel eyed the both of them with a cocky smirk. "Lucky you two didn't fall with something."

Tristan tried to fight his grin while Miels frowned. "Baby, stop it. I'm all yours. I certainly don't want to remember that past."

She gave him a chaste kiss. "Good. Now let's continue."

Miels started, "Logun's Lemon sickness. Dated one hundred and fifty years ago in the Island. A man named Logun didn't realize he'd fertilized a tree of lemons with the wrong stuff. All of the lemons came out bad and made people sick. Easily curable with a sorcerer..."

SPARRING WITH NORYA was just the distraction Tristan needed after being cooped up in that room all day discussing all sorts of plagues and sicknesses that had run through the lands. He especially needed this distraction after hearing two more whoring sicknesses from Miels.

Fighting with Norya was unlike any training he ever had with the other guards. She was just as great a fighter as any of them, so it wasn't about the skill. It was how much fun Tristan found it to kick her ass.

Or how much fun it was when she kicked his ass.

They normally both walked away limping and bruised up.

Today wouldn't be any different. They prepared, circling one another on the mat as a few guards stood around watching. Apparently, it was amusing to watch them because of how unused to seeing a woman fight they were. Especially a woman fight as brutally as the men because though Evony and Gemma could fight, they were never as harsh as Norya was on these mats.

Tristan's fists were up as he smirked. "Are we scared, little warrior?"

"You tell me." She smirked back. "Afraid a girl is going to beat you?"

His lips upturned into a grin. "You love to bait me, don't you?" he responded before attacking.

Norya blocked as Tristan punched at her gut, then threw her own fists.

They were fast, hitting and blocking and kicking and moving around the mat. Their grunts filled the space past the guards making bets around them. So far in the three months Norya had been at the palace, they'd fought nearly four dozen times, with Norya winning those odds by a slight margin. The boys had come up with the bets the second time he and Norya sparred, and they'd enjoyed making money from Norya and Tristan's fun ever since.

Norya's fist landed its hit against Tristan's jaw, and his entire face throbbed with the pain.

"You're going to pay for that tonight, my little whore," he mumbled as he kicked her feet from under her and caught her in a deadlock. He locked his arms tight enough to nearly cut off her oxygen.

Her elbow flew back to land a hit into his stomach, but Tristan didn't let go.

"Call it, and I'll let you breathe again."

She held out for as long as she could, but finally she stomped on the ground in their decisive move that meant they were forfeiting.

Some cheers bellowed through the training room around some grumbles as Tristan released Norya and allowed her to breathe once more. He smirked as the men around him started talking of wins and losses.

"Maybe I need to prepare more tasks for you men if you have all the time in the day to mess around here." Sparrow's dark and brooding voice filled the space.

The men scurried with his presence, moving about their evenings.

"Spoilsport," Tristan teased the man.

Norya tried to fight her amusement as she eyed Sparrow. "I thought your wife was meant to make you less grumpy?"

"She has," Tristan and Sparrow said at once.

Norya whistled. "Not much that I've seen."

Sparrow gave her an annoyed look, then turned an equally annoyed, yet more pissed, look on Tristan.

"What?" Tristan stood straighter.

"Do you know how many complaints I've gotten of the staff walking in on you two? No one cares if you fuck, but stop being so reckless about it. The help is scared to walk into rooms lest they catch you two. You're in the North, not the Island. Act like it."

Tristan raised his hands in the defensive. "Sorry, Spar. We'll be more careful, mate."

Sparrow's jaw locked in place as he walked out of the room.

Tristan watched him go, upset that his actions had obviously been so much that the servants—who never complained—had begun doing so.

When he turned to Norya, that thought left him completely because she was smirking, a shimmer in her eyes. She had a way of doing that—making all of his thoughts disappear until she was all that belonged. Until she made up every bit of chemistry that his mind rolled through his body. "What?"

"*You're* going to be more careful?"

Tristan moved for her, delighted as she moved backward until her back hit the wall. "What makes you think I wouldn't be?"

"Being born in the North means nothing, spy. You're basically an Islander."

He chuckled in that deep way he knew made her pussy wet. His nose skimmed down her jaw until he reached her ear. "Maybe you're right." His arms caged her in. "And if I'm an Islander, then I take my pleasure whenever I wish for it." He skimmed his nose across her jaw to the opposite ear. "So get on your knees."

Her gaze lit up with delight as she slipped down the wall, never breaking eye contact.

Her hands skimmed up his thighs until they reached the ties to his trousers, then loosened them only enough to take his cock out. Then her mouth was hungrily taking him, wetting him with her spit and gagging as his cock fucked the back of her throat.

"That's right, baby," Tristan taunted as a hand dropped to

take her hair into his fist. "Take it all the way back. That's right. Good job, little whore."

She moaned around his cock, spit and pre-cum falling out of her mouth as she continued to take him as far back as she could.

"Good j—" Tristan was cut off when something hit the back of his head, and a growl filled the room.

When he turned, he met Sparrow's deathly gaze, and couldn't help himself but smirk.

Sparrow slammed the door on his way out with a grumbled "I'm going to kill you."

Tristan laughed as he turned back to meet Norya's gaze. There was amusement in her eyes too as she continued to take him far back in her throat.

He pulled on her hair. "You got me in trouble." He thrust his cock deeper into her throat. "I think you need to pay for that."

She tried to smile around his cock as her hands played with his balls. She looked amazing in that moment. Made him want this with her, and only her, every day. He had a feeling telling her to get on her knees daily wouldn't be too difficult.

Before long, he was at that beautiful precipice, balls heavy with the need to fill her, all of her.

He came into her mouth, his own mouth watering at the look of his cum dripping out from her lips.

He wiped at her mouth, then brought the cum-stained fingers to her tongue for her lick off. "Good job, my filthy little whore."

CHAPTER 7
TRISTAN

As part of regular physical upkeep, most everyone at the palace, but especially the guards and hunters, ran rounds around the grounds. It kept up their stamina and endurance and was an integral part of staying alive in dangerous situations.

But it was never a part of the trainings. Everyone was allowed to do so as often as they liked and at whatever hour. Tristan's favorite time to do so was dusk. Even in this autumn weather with the colder breeze, it was worth it to be out on the grounds and witness the sun going down. It was also nice to feel the crunch of the orange leaves beneath his steps.

On top of all that, most everyone did their runs in the mornings so he was almost always left to his thoughts. His thoughts, the impending storm, and the beautiful skies, what could be better?

"Are the common folk in the North truly so sad? That you could go so slow and keep pace with them running away from you? Or after you?" Norya's voice clouded his peace.

"I was having a relaxing moment to myself."

"I just wanted to make sure you were getting the proper cardio in. I need a man with stamina."

Tristan quirked a brow as they jogged side by side. "I don't think your body will be able to take any more stamina. You can barely take what I give you now."

"Mm. And there's no way I fake that to give you confidence."

He laughed. Norya was so different from any woman he knew.

Or maybe she wasn't. Maybe it was just something about being around her that made the things she said sexy. Hell, Tristan could imagine her saying 'moldy carcasses are smelling up the village' in a sexy way.

"What do you want, barbarianette?"

"Just getting my run in. Like you. I won't bother your concentration. Get lost in your thoughts."

"Then why come up to me?"

"We can enjoy each other's companionship and not speak, spy. We've certainly done it before."

She was right. And not merely because of sex. Plenty of time in the past few months, they'd been together and not said a thing to the other. When he was reading missives in his suite and she was cleaning her weapons beside him. When they were in trainings—not the times they fooled around, but during real trainings. When they simply sat together and watched the skies or listened to one of the women in the Posse tell a story or the way a guard would blush over speaking to a beautiful servant.

So Tristan turned back to look at the beautiful skies and enjoyed the crunch of the leaves underfoot.

But like all those moments with Norya, he couldn't shake the knowledge that she was right beside him. He was always aware when she was in his vicinity.

She was certainly physically eye-catching, but because of the releases she allowed him to get, that wasn't the distracting part. It was everything else—her.

They'd spent time together every day for three months, and in that time, Tristan had come to learn nearly all there was to know about her. From her orphanage—which surprisingly didn't have a sad story behind it—to her first time holding a bow and arrow to her first kiss. And still, he felt like he'd only scratched the surface of all things Norya.

To be fair, he'd been friends with Miels and Sparrow for two decades and still, there were things the three of them didn't know of one another. It was the exciting part of relationships—always having more to learn about the other.

Tristan had certainly loved learning what his brothers were like when they fell in love, and somehow, they'd both gone and done so at the same time. He loved seeing the personalities of their women and how it perfectly countered their own. Loved seeing them taken down a few pegs and especially loved getting them in trouble with their wives.

It was astonishing. How, even after two decades, Tristan still felt like his relationship with his brothers was growing every day. He loved those fuckers.

Crunching of leaves not made by his feet brought him out of his thoughts. When he glanced her way, she was already watching him. "What?"

"Nothing," she answered. "You looked over at the same moment I happened to."

Norya never lied about things like that. She didn't see the point behind it. She always said if one had feelings, it didn't make sense to bottle them up. It was the nice thing about being friends-with-benefits with her—Tristan could be sure nothing more was ever happening.

"You're distracting me," he said because although he'd

been able to get lost in his thoughts, it wasn't the same. He was too aware of her presence.

"I haven't done a thing. If you're thinking about me, that's your fault."

"It's a little hard not to think about you when you're running right beside me."

"Not true. I was just thinking about the toffee cake I had after breakfast this morning."

"And that made you look at me?"

"I was wondering if I could get some more. Then I thought, of course I can, I'm sleeping with a Posse spy. Then I figured I could just get you to get it for me."

He laughed—laughed. In any other situation, he would be annoyed. But with Norya, he laughed.

SPENDING time with Miels and Sparrow had always been Tristan's favorite pasttime. Then when James came into the mix, things only became more fun. Norya had now taken up that spot. He couldn't believe he'd let her run with him. The guys knew never to try joining him while he was doing his laps. But with Norya, he didn't seem to mind her company.

He knew, too, that Norya wouldn't take advantage of the privilege of running with him that afternoon. She'd have fun sometimes but would respect his alone time. The guys would've done that too, but it didn't feel the same. Something about having Norya around *was* relaxing.

Though he loved his time with the boys and his friendship with Norya, he'd come to favor a time with two people in particular above all of them, as long as he got those moments in small doses.

Evony and Gemma were firecrackers, but something about being with them made Tristan feel like he was being teased and loved on by sisters. He'd always wanted that—sisters.

One was shamelessly loud, bright and full of life. The other sweeter and more quiet, which somehow made her the more devious of the two. They had somehow become some of Tristan's favorite people.

Though Ro was like a sister, Eve and Gem truly acted like it. Or what he imagined sisters acted like. Tristan wouldn't give up spending time with them for the world... though he could imagine a certain barbarianette luring him away.

They were in Evony and Sparrow's suite, seated on the couch with either woman beside him, while they tried to teach Tristan how to sew since they were working on their own projects. It wasn't a skill he rather cared for, but if it meant spending time with them, then he didn't care.

Evony laughed. "You're quite awful at this, Tris."

"Yeah, yeah, yeah." Tristan laughed along as he tried again to get the needle where he wanted it. It wasn't his fault the damn thing kept finding its way to another part of the cloth. "How about I take you two out for a sparring match, and we'll see how great you are then." Much better than most women, even plenty of men, that was the answer.

Gemma answered around their laughs. "Please do. I suspect you'll have maybe twenty minutes at most before the news spreads and our husbands come to hunt you down."

He rolled his eyes, focusing on the needle and cloth in his hands. "Your husbands can kiss my ass."

Evony threw her work—which was perfectly done—onto the table before them. "If you're not afraid of our husbands, let's go!"

Tristan met her gaze and read what she truly meant—*if*

you're not afraid of what the Master Assassin will do to you if you lay a finger on me, then let's spar.

"Sorry. Can't spar pregnant women."

"Okay. We'll put it in the books for six months from now. Then both of us would've given birth." Gemma smiled.

He could agree to save face, but he knew these girls' memories. They'd find him in exactly six months time and make him keep his word. He could already imagine Evony's magic forcing him to stay in the private training room while they allowed the rumor to spread that he was sparring them. James and Sparrow would kill him. "You guys are really annoying, you know that?"

He was focused on his work again when he got a sloppy kiss on either cheek and arms circling him.

"Aw," Evony teased in a voice she'd use on a child. "We're sorry, little Tristan."

"Very, very sorry," Gemma added in the same tone.

"Assholes. The both of you."

They laughed as they pulled away and continued on with their work. He was trying to sew his name into the cloth but was too in thought to give the work the attention it required. Because he didn't get the time to think things through on his run, it was hard not to let his mind run now. Even though Norya had been quiet enough for a large part of their run, Tristan had been too distracted with her presence.

He thought about his relationship with the women in his life. There was Rosaelia, his Princess. She was the first female relationship he'd ever had after Ed adopted him and Miels into the family years ago. She was a babe when he'd come into the picture and had always grown up as a sister.

Or maybe a cousin because he wasn't as close to her as he was to these girls beside him.

For years, that was it. He'd never fallen in love, had crushes but never love, and all of the sex had been just that. Sex.

Then Evony and Gemma moved to the palace and he had these other women about. Yet never did he think about screwing either one of them. Understandably as when they met, the rings on Gemma and James's fingers indicated she was taken, and the shock of seeing Ro's face on Eve's was too much to the system.

But even after that, when Evony wasn't yet possessed by Sparrow and her personality had wholly differentiated her from the Princess, it never happened.

Yet on the contrary, when he went out for a screw, he never felt the need for more than an orgasm or two. Never wanted more from the women and left before they could try to get more from him.

Then there was Norya.

In the Island, it'd been a fun idea to screw her because fuck, she was sexy, but he hadn't expected to love talking to her too. It'd started with a case of they were living together in the nonas' home so he couldn't simply run away, then turned into this friendship. All because *she* hadn't wanted more. In fact, she'd been as adamant as him that it remain sexual, so their friendship had been given the opportunity to blossom. And they found that their personalities meshed so well it felt impossible to be away from one another for too long.

Maybe that was why he could be friends-with-benefits with her and nobody else. They were too similar.

And while he loved the other women in his life, they weren't quite like him. These two women beside him were some of his favorite people to exist yet he'd always been able to tell that they were meant for his friends, that his relationships with them would grow because they made his friends happy. It wasn't like that with Nor.

Evony looked down at the handkerchief in his hands. "You're destroying the poor thing."

Tristan huffed as he came out of his thoughts, and finally threw the thing onto the table beside Evony's work as his hand moved for her belly. "Your mama thinks she's so funny."

Before he could truly touch her, she pushed his hand away. "Oh, stop it. You can barely even tell yet."

Tristan narrowed his green orbs. "You know, it's quite obvious that's Spar's baby in you because you're a lot grumpier now. Turning into your husband?"

Evony only smirked, her blue eyes shining with love and pride. It was the same pride that sparked in Sparrow's eyes when speaking of his little family. This was what had kept Tristan away from seducing the Magician from the beginning —somehow knowing Evony was meant for his brother.

Tristan rolled his eyes, turning to Gemma instead. As his hand landed on her bigger stomach, he leaned into her. "Your mama's much nicer, little Southerner."

Gemma's hand landed over his as a small kick hit him. "Oh, look at that!" She laughed. "Little Southerner is excited about his Uncle Tristan."

Tristan gave Evony a cocky grin. "Of course he is."

Evony rolled her eyes. "Little Southerner is a cheeky little thing like his parents." Her hands rested on her barely there bump. "Little Sparrow, on the other hand, already doesn't like you, like *his* parents."

Tristan's arm wrapped around Evony's neck and brought her into his side as he leaned closer to Gemma, all three laughing in hysterics. "You think you're real funny, don't you, Eve?"

CHAPTER 8
NORYA

She felt slightly guilty breaking in on Tristan's private time on the run. Slightly, only because she didn't plan on doing so again. At least not often.

But guilty because she prized her own alone time and hoped no one would ruin it.

As she ogled Tristan's ass as he made his way to the King's wing to shower before dinner, Norya smiled to herself. She planned on biting that scrumptious bit of him tonight. Her teeth marks would look especially pretty on his ass.

Before any of that, before she could head in for her own shower before dinner, Norya turned to the cottage at the edge of the woods. It was where Gabriel, the stablehand Ashtyn was into, lived.

Two other stablehands also had cottages at the edge of the palace greens rather than living in the palace, but both of those were on the other side of the palace. Gabriel's home was alone out there, but it looked quaint, comfortable, just what the grouchy healer would need at the end of a long day of dealing with morons. Her words completely. Norya wasn't entirely sure healers were meant to speak of their patients like that, but it made her laugh.

When she reached the cottage, Gabriel was on one side, shirtless as he and another stablehand Norya recognized as Dale, chopped at wood. "You two should do this on the other side of your cottage. Give the women at the palace something to ogle."

They both turned quickly with her ambush, then smiled at her words. Dale was a little bit taller than Gabriel but both towered over her. Dale's hair was black and choppy whereas Gabriel's was a rich chocolate and floppy. Dale's eyes were blue whereas Gabriel's were chestnut brown. But both wore charming smiles.

Norya swore it was a prerequisite to becoming a stablehand at this palace.

"What may we do for you, Miss Islander?" Dale asked, bowing as a way to tease her because they all knew she didn't consider herself any higher than them.

"I wanted to talk to you about the horses and weapons," Norya answered, though she was speaking more to Gabriel.

He dropped his axe and grabbed for his towel to dry off the sweat. Now that they weren't exerting all that energy, he and Dale would need to put clothes on to fight this autumn chill. "What about them?"

"You guys normally prepare the horses for swords more than any other weapon, right?"

"Yes. That is the main weapon here."

"What's your policy for a bow and arrow?"

"This sounds like a conversation you two can have," Dale said, then turned back to chopping at the wood. They already had a nice pile, but growing up in the Island had taught Norya one very important thing—there could never be too much chopped wood.

Gabriel led Norya inside, where the hearth was flickering and keeping the space warm. "I don't know if we have one really. At least, not since I've been here, and I've been here for ten years."

"Can we make it happen?"

"Of course. I'll talk to Papa Ignatius, see if we had anything already. But it cannot be too difficult to incorporate. It will be almost like storing any other weapon. That is, I'm given to understand you're asking because you don't want to carry the weapon on your back?"

"And for any extras. I know that's what you normally do for the swords, but since I'm much better with the bow, I'd like an extra one for my horse."

"Do you have plans to go anywhere?"

"No." Not yet. But eventually. Norya wanted to see the lands, discover new spots that become her favorite.

Gabriel only nodded. He didn't pry into why she would want a way to store weapons if she wasn't going anywhere. Norya appreciated that.

"I'll look into it. It's likely only going to be a different pack to tie to your horse. If that's the case, I'll begin working on the needed pieces for you."

She quirked a brow. "You can make things out of leather too?"

"Too?"

She smiled. "You did a bit of woodwork in the Island." She still remembered the piece he made when he was silently sitting in on their 'meetings.' He'd left it in the house, the one Killian had gifted to Clark for saving Sael from those men at the whorehouse. It was a nice decorative piece for the house and somehow made the place feel even more lived in.

His returning grin was endearing. "Then yes. I do leather work too."

"That's kinda sexy."

He laughed. "Thank you."

"But you don't care that I find what you do sexy. Or that I might find you sexy?" He was, but not in the way that would make her hot. He was simply objectively hot.

"No."

"Ah, what a lucky girl Ashtyn is."

He still grinned, but there was more sadness in his eyes now. "Why don't you tell her that?"

"She knows. She just likes to see people suffer. You know, for a healer, your woman is quite the bitch."

His head fell back as a loud bark of laughter left him. "I know."

Her lips tipped up softly watching him.

"What?"

"I always liked observing claimed couples on the Island. It's harder to do so here because of how reserved everyone is—though the Posse's comfortability with each other makes things easier—"

"Especially with how unreserved Evony, Gemma, and James can be?"

She laughed. "Yes. But in terms of other couples, you Northerners are so much more reserved. And I'm not even talking about doing it in public. That was never the part I was into anyway. I mean, watching claimed couples fall for each other. I still see it here, but it's not as blatant all the time. I just like that with you, it is. You don't care to hide your feelings."

"Makes me kinda stupid, huh? A masochist? She keeps rejecting me, and I keep coming back for more?"

Norya shrugged. "I told you. She's a bitch."

"I feel like I shouldn't let you talk about her like that."

She laughed. "As you wish." As she turned to leave, Norya paused and turned for him. "Thanks for the help with the weapons. And... wait just a little more. I know she won't be able to resist much longer."

He winked. "I'm ready to wait an eternity."

Norya left with a smile. It was harder to see claimed couples in the North, but watching Gabriel's feelings on his sleeve, her heart grew warm. He deserved every happiness.

CHAPTER 9
NORYA

Her breaths came out roughly as she fell to her back on the bed.

Her times with Tristan were always invigorating, but damn, that was amazing. Her vision was still trying to come back from the stars.

A grin rose on her lips, both from the incredible sex and because she could hear Tristan's equally out-of-breath self beside her. "That was supposed to tire us out, Tris. My body's dead, but my mind is wide awake."

"Mine too." He threw his body to the side like it took more energy than it should to turn and face her. "Talk to me. Tell me those pretty little secrets to put me to sleep, Nor."

She snorted. "My secrets put you to sleep, asshole?"

He yawned, obviously faked as he never tried to be a very good actor with her. "So very boring, barbarianette."

"If they're so boring, then you tell me one of yours. Let's see how exciting yours are."

He gave a cheeky little laugh as he closed his eyes, smile

disappearing as he said, "I was the one who found my parents on the brink of death."

"The brink of death? I thought they were dead and that's why you had to go scavenging?"

He tsked. "Brink of dead. Everyone thinks they were dead, but they weren't. I don't think it's possible that a healer could've saved them, but who knows. I think had there been a healer like Ash—one who was basically a Master—then maybe."

Norya took in his features. He still looked relaxed, like telling his story wasn't a big deal even though apparently no one else knew of it. "What happened?"

"I'm lying." He paused, then explained, "They definitely could've been healed. Or cared for, I think. They were alert enough to speak to me. Maybe as long as there was a good medic around, they'd be cared for enough. Maybe go more peacefully, under remedies."

"What'd they say?" That they loved him? That they didn't want this to be the last thing he saw? That everything would be all right, sweet boy?

"They told me to hurry up and get the medic. That they couldn't believe how unlucky they were that I hadn't been home when the attack happened because as adults, they could survive it, but as a child, I wouldn't have."

Her gasp was involuntary. She was from the Island, used to the more savage way of life. Yet it still shocked her to hear this. Maybe because she always assumed Northern and Southerners to be soft. So soft they could never hurt their own children, ever wish them harm. Even Islanders didn't normally hurt their own.

He gave a slight shrug, eyes still closed. "It'd been all I was used to from them. The others around town? They were sweet on me. I think that was my saving grace, that those neighbors showed me that I could be… I don't know. Pleasant? But yeah, my parents, not great. Ed and the others know that much, but not exactly how they died."

"And how'd they die?"

"They were laid out on the ground, blood gushing, intestines showing. Honestly, it was vile. But they were defenseless. I thought about leaving them like that, waiting for them to bleed out, but I had just got back from the festival in the neighboring town and when the others got back to their homes, they'd be able to hear them screaming for help. I didn't want to allow the chance for them to make it out alive. So I grabbed the fire iron by the mantel and… I started with my mother. She was less vile with me, so I gave her the chance to go first, faster. A simple slash through the heart. My father… he made sure never to leave scars. He was smart like that. He knew the neighbors loved me too much to allow me to get hurt, so he never scarred me. But there're all sorts of things to be done that don't leave scars. He threatened to kill those neighbors who were sweet on me if I told them, so I kept quiet. I wanted him to see his wife die, then to feel the pain some more before he was gone.

"I… burned the fire iron in the flames, then brought it to him. He yelled at me, still cursing me instead of begging for forgiveness. Luckily, I had come home a bit earlier than the neighbors, so I knew I had some time. I was only a boy, so I didn't necessarily have the strength to saw through his leg, but I tried. Realistically, I only made it deep enough to shatter bones, then tried far too hard to pull the thing back out. He screamed from the pain but never stopped harassing me. Eventually I got the thing out and through his hand and gut too, before I was too tired to try for any more. I stabbed him through the heart and left the thing there. I had blood all over me, but it wasn't a thought. Everyone assumed I had come in, found them like that, rushed to their sides where I got the blood on me, then run out for help. After that, I wanted to stick around because the neighbors were so good, but I felt guilty constantly looking those people I truly cherished in the eyes and constantly lying to them. I found Miels after that, then Ed not long after, and I had a new life."

She tentatively reached a hand out for him, not knowing what to touch. "I don't think Ed or any of the Posse would judge you for it."

"I know. I just... like keeping it to myself."

Her fingers chose his lips to play with. "Why are you telling me this?"

"You're my best friend."

"Miels was your best friend before me."

His eyes remained closed, but his lips twitched up. "You're my best best friend."

She let out an airy laugh. "A story to beat that? I don't think I have one."

"Good. I don't want you to beat it. I hope, even growing and fending for yourself in the Island, that life wasn't as grim with you."

That was sweet. Sweet spy Tristan. Sometimes she could forget how nice he was because of the things he did to her body.

So she decided to give him a different kind of story. "I once cried when the sweets were given to the eight-year-old boy instead of me even though we both tied in a gathering contest."

The desired effect took place, and Tristan laughed. "That's normal. All kids get jealous, especially if you tied."

"I was sixteen!"

His eyes snapped open, and he broke out laughing. "Sixteen?"

"Shut up." She smacked him.

Instead of flying off the bed as she'd hoped her hit would cause, he wrapped his arm around her waist and pulled her in close. "Oh, I'm never letting you forget it. *Sixteen!*"

"And that's a story *I* never tell people. It's embarrassing, and I'm already regretting telling you."

"Tough. I don't think I can ever forget it." He smirked. "What kind of sweets?"

"Gumyons."

"Gumyons? Isn't that a Southern sweet?"

"Which is why they were prized! And if we tied, then the sweets should've been broken up between the two of us! But they figured as a child tying a teenager, technically that made him the better gatherer." Because pity prizes weren't a thing. No child would ever be prized simply because they were a child. No participation prizes. None of the lands worked like that, but especially not the Island.

He brought her under his chin, one hand holding her still as the other ran a soothing hand down her hair. "Okay, Norya darling. Whatever you say."

"I'm just say—"

"Shh, sleep time, Norya darling, sleep time."

She wanted to punch him, but couldn't help her giggles. At least it helped dissipate the funk of talking about his parents.

Around the giggles, while shoved into his chest, Norya mumbled, "Asshole."

CHAPTER 10
TRISTAN

"I've spoken with Ashtyn," Sparrow added to the end of their usual palace matters meeting as they all sat in Edmund's suite.

Edmund was in his usual spot by the fire, Sparrow across from him while he stared into the flames he seemed to like more since Evony came into his life. Miels and James shared the other side of Edmund's couch while Tristan lounged in an armchair across from them. To finish off the group, Killian remained standing, prowling from one end of the room to the other like the barbarian in him couldn't remain sitting.

"And what did she have to say?" Edmund asked as the storm outside got louder, banging against the windows to his suite.

"She cares too much about what might happen to the public, so if her skills are required, she will allow for it to become public knowledge, allow for others to find out about her, and possibly title her a Master."

"If her skills are required?" Killian asked.

"Yes. We'll need to check out this plague. Make sure that it truly is something requiring a Master. Otherwise, there would be no reason to put so many eyes on her. The girl deserves to keep her privacy, and unlike our Magician, she will not be able to hide it. Even not being named a Master, she'll have too many eyes on her as someone close to Masterhood."

Miels nodded. "We've got a list of plagues and sicknesses that could be similar. We'll finish up the research on those specific ones." The ones that had been placed in the *Possibility* column when going over all of their findings. They'd been spending their time doing extra research on those since that meeting.

Sparrow met their gazes. "Okay. Then we'll see if heading up north is required."

They all agreed and moved to leave the suite. Most of them had women to get to, and the two of them who didn't—he and Edmund—had other matters they could take care of. Or Ed could steal Ro and Tristan Eve from the others and watch them go berserk. The thought made him smile. That definitely sounded far more amusing than being holed up in the library.

They were out in the King's wing hall when Evony's door opened and four women tumbled out, voices overtaking one another, so nothing said was discernible. What was quite obvious though was that Norya was trying to run away from all the hands coming at her.

"Hold still, Norya. You look lovely," a woman Tristan recognized as a tailor's assistant argued with the barbarianette as two other sets of hands grabbed her.

"I *look* ridiculous," Norya argued.

She looked beautiful. Stunning. His body buzzed at the sight.

"No, you don't." Gemma played with her hair, tucking a strand that'd come loose from the usual braid behind her ear.

As the chuckles came from their group, all four women's

eyes were on them as they realized they weren't alone in the hall.

Evony gave that devious smile. "How does she look, boys? Honestly."

She was in a dress, one finely made for everyday wear, like she was one of the Princesses. Though like Evony, it was unlikely to see her in it often. It was tight on top, showing her breasts beautifully, and slightly flowy on the bottom. It dropped to her feet, and Tristan imagined would make it difficult for her to run or do any sort of fighting comfortably.

It would make any man drop to his knees, though no other man needed to drop to their knees for her. He would be taking care of that issue.

"Stunning," a voice came from behind him.

"Beautiful." Another.

"Breathtaking." Another one.

"Ridiculous." Killian's tone held a laugh within it.

"Thank you." Norya pointed to her brother. "I look, *and feel*, ridiculous."

Rosaelia popped out of the room. "She does not look ridiculous!"

Killian's eyes widened like he hadn't known she'd be there, and was now worried he was in big trouble.

"Why would you say that, Kill?" she continued to berate her husband. "She looks stunning, and just because you guys are barbarians doesn't mean she cannot wear a dress. As if a fine dress makes one look ridiculous." She crossed her arms before her chest. "Is that what you truly think of me? Ridiculous in my dresses?"

Killian's head shook the entire time. "No, princess." When she went to argue some more, he stepped forward. "No, no, no, I'm sorry. I didn't mean it." He met Norya's eyes. "You look amazing."

Norya rolled those beautiful dark orbs. "Whipped shit."

Rosaelia huffed and moved back into her sister's suite. Killian gave a merciful look to Evony, who only laughed as he followed after his girl.

"Tris," Gemma called in that lovely voice of hers. "How does she look?"

"I think she looks beautiful, Gem. I just don't understand why she's wearing it."

The tailor's assistant whipped around to give him a death glare. "Because every woman deserves a dress she feels breath-taking in."

He held up his hands in the defensive. "Agreed. But, if I may, she doesn't look to feel beautiful in it. And it's not who she is. The little barbarianette feels more comfortable hunting and dirty than poised and proper." Though he could imagine a few dresses she might like herself in.

His cock was growing hard thinking of her in those dresses. Ones too short to be decent for anyone's eyes but his.

"Thank you!" Norya cried. "Someone on my side! This is why you're my best friend."

Tristan's lips twitched into a laugh he fought as he winked at her. "Anything for my best friend."

The tailor huffed in disappointment.

"It's okay, Atiana," Evony soothed. "She's only been here three months. We'll get her obsessed with gowns by the year mark. It took me some time too." Then she muttered, "Though I was never as difficult to please.

Atiana smiled and looked absolutely stunning. "I'll make it my mission."

"Can I take this off now?" Norya grumbled.

"Wait!" Gemma caught her before Norya could run off and turned to Edmund. "What do you think, Your Highness? She make a nice addition to the Posse?"

Norya grumbled as her eyes hit the back of her head.

Edmund laughed from beside Tristan. "She looks amazing. The dress, like all of the dresses made by Miss. Bonèmere, would make any man fall to his knees."

Atiana's cheeks bloomed a deep red as her gaze turned to Edmund, the man seeming like he was attempting his hardest to not keep his eyes glued to her.

As the only man without a woman, Tristan realized the others were too preoccupied with eyeing their other halves to notice, but he wasn't blind—his King had his eyes set on the little tailor's assistant, even if he tried not to.

And from the looks of it, his feelings were reciprocated.

Tristan smacked Edmund in the back to get him out of the haze of staring at the beautiful woman as he leaned in to whisper, "I will go record this date and time as the first moment I have witnessed you interested in another."

Edmund's dark orbs snapped to his. "What?"

Tristan's eyes shot to the side as if pointing to Atiana. "She obviously wants you too. But tell me, is this a secret you two have been hiding that even *Sparrow* didn't find out or are you being too stupid to do anything about your desires?"

Edmund's glare was piercing. "I am your King, Tristan."

"So send me to the dungeons." His lips tipped up. "But first, answer my question—have you had her yet?"

Edmund's dark orbs shot back to where the girl was standing, and when Tristan turned to look, Atiana gave Edmund a final longing look before heading into Evony's suite after the others.

"By the way she looks at you, I take it you haven't done a thing about it," Tristan concluded. "I can't understand why. She's beautiful. Surely every man here has an eye on her. If we didn't have the no palace women rule, I'd have an eye on he—"

Edmund had his shirt fisted, and him thrown into the wall

so quickly, Tristan couldn't think to defend himself. "You will not touch her."

Tristan smirked as James and Sparrow's heads popped out of the room to see what was happening. A second later, Miels was there, all eyeing them curiously. The King had never been so testy as to throw any of them into a wall. He was the most patient man alive.

"I had no intentions of touching her. I have my fuck buddy," Tristan whispered so the others didn't hear. "But I thought you should be made aware that my love for you would've stopped me from going after her even if I didn't have Nor, but most of the men here won't think like that. Especially if they do not know of your desires."

Edmund ground his jaw and stepped away. He shook out his arms, then turned to head down the hall and to lords knew where. Probably to exercise the adrenaline out of his body.

Tristan met the gazes of the three other men in the Posse and shook his head. If Edmund had been keeping this part of him a secret, Tristan would respect that. He only wondered how long until he could no longer take it.

Tristan chuckled to himself, then turned his thoughts back to those daydreams of Norya in short dresses he needed to make a reality.

CHAPTER II

NORYA

"Are you hiding, barbarianette?" A body plopped down beside her, legs falling through the railings. "Trying to become a homemaker, are we?"

Norya smiled down at her fabrics and thread and needle. "And what's wrong with that? That's probably the hardest job."

"Absolutely nothing. You can make my home any day of the week."

She rolled her eyes. "What do you want, Tristan? I'm trying to relax."

"And my body does things to you that don't make that possible?" He smirked.

"Sure. Let's say that."

"Well you interrupted my time alone. I figured I'd return the favor."

She scoffed. "I knew that was gonna bite me in the ass."

He tsked as he leaned into her, nose skimming her from shoulder to neck. "That's my job."

Norya pricked her finger trying to get the needle she was

working with through the fabric. She growled and pushed Tristan away. "You're distracting my work, Tris. I didn't do that to you."

She didn't have to turn her eyes away from the work in her lap to know he'd rolled his eyes.

"Fine, I'll behave," he grumbled as he fell back to lie on the ground.

They remained in silence for some time, the only reminder of the disturbance to her privacy was Tristan's leg hitting hers where they floated in the air. She didn't mind it though. It was nice, comforting to have him beside her as she tried to teach herself this skill.

He behaved so well, never growing too bored and breaking out into conversation, that finally, Norya was the one to break the silence. "Have you guys considered it could be something in nature that is causing the sickness?"

"We have," he answered, but didn't sit back up. "It would have to be something ingested though because the plague isn't contagious. And if that is the case, then it must either be something native to only the northern parts of the North, or whatever plant they're harvesting from is tainted. That would be the optimistic outcome, I guess. Because then it means someone isn't purposefully poisoning their peers."

Norya turned to him. He was still lying on his back, and he had an arm draped over his eyes. He looked relaxed and like he was preparing for a nap. Why wouldn't he be? He took control of his life, could choose when to do things, what he wanted to do with life. She was still too new to the North to get the answer to any of those questions.

"If you find out Ashtyn is needed, can I come to wherever she needs to travel?"

His arm moved up and an eye popped open. "Getting bored stifled in the palace?"

She shrugged. "You get to go on your checks. The most I get is going hunting and while I love it, I want to get out more. See more of the North. See the South." That night to the tavern had been the one escapade around the North, and she wanted more, wanted to explore.

He sat back up so their faces were close. "I imagine as an Islander not allowed to these lands, I would feel the same way." He pinched her nose. "Of course you can come. You're an amazing warrior and you can help keep us fed if we ever need to hunt a small meal for ourselves."

"Does that happen often?"

"No, but from time to time."

Norya dropped her things to the side and turned fully for Tristan, bringing her legs from where they were dangling to hug into her chest. She smiled at the prospect of getting to see more of the lands. "I know we'd be going for the plague, but I still want to see some of your favorite places if we're anywhere near them!"

His grin cracked over his features as he rose to stand. Taking her hand, he led her to the window only a few feet from where they were sat and placed her body before his. He pointed to some peaks far off in the distance. "You can't see them much from here, but there're some smaller mountains to the west of the lands, half in the South, half in the North. That's my most favored of places. It won't be on the travels for the plague, but I'll take you there after."

Her answering smile was soft. "I don't know how sexy it'd be to watch you fall from some hills, Tris."

He bit the back of her neck instead of answering. "How sexy would it be if I pushed you from the top."

She laughed as she pushed him away, moving for the stairs to the bottom of the library. "Whatever, spy. I'm from the Island. *You* certainly don't scare me."

"Is that so?" he asked with a smirk as he followed her down.

When she reached the bottom and turned to meet his gaze, green orbs stared down at her, glinting, and there was mischief written all over his features.

Norya backed away, smacking a table as she moved, and prepared to make a run for it. His legs were so much longer though, so she wasn't sure she'd be able to get away. She might have to beat him in the middle of the library. "Behave, spy."

"Heed your own advice, barbarianette," he muttered as he lunged.

At the move, Norya let out a squeal she wasn't aware could come from her, and ran. He chased her up one stack of shelves and down another until they were back by the tables. Tristan pushed a table to get to her, causing the thing to screech and two books to tumble off.

Norya was giggling—giggling—when he caught her.

"The little barbarianette is in trouble now," he teased into her neck.

She was still giggling when they heard grumbling coming from upstairs as the door that led to the keepers' offices rattled. "What the hell are you kids doing?"

They met one another wide-eyed, and Tristan pulled her fast so they could hide. The childishness of running to the back corner to hide behind some shelves only made her giggle more.

"Shh." His finger trapped her lips together. "You're going to get us caught."

There was no reason for them to hide in the first place. As part of the Posse, they wouldn't be reprimanded for their fooling around, but Norya appreciated that Tristan still made them do so. Both because she didn't want more talk around the palace about how much she didn't fit into their ways, but also because this was far more exciting. She'd never felt this light before.

Norya trapped her lips together to keep the giggles in, and they both listened out for Lori, the keeper who had come out of her office expecting one of her kids to have been the cause of the ruckus.

"Which one of you kids was it?" the woman asked the air as she picked the dropped books from the ground and placed them on the table. By the screech that came next, she then moved the table back the couple of inches to its spot.

Lori's mumbles to herself continued—probably about how those kids were always running around playing catch—as she hopefully began to leave.

Norya took the time to examine Tristan. He was tall, built, not as goofy as Miels but a cheekiness still filled him, especially around her. He was almost too handsome to be real and a perfect listener for when she needed someone to talk to. He knew exactly how to be rough with her in bed, but also how to take things slow, simply hold her, other times.

She moved his finger from her mouth and rose to her tiptoes to kiss the corner of his lips. "You have a tiny scar under that stubble. Did you know that?" she whispered.

"Mm." His nose played with hers, their mouths brushing together. "Not many people do."

His eyes were a shining green, bright and alive, mischievous and inviting.

Norya was pretty sure their little library visitor was gone now and they could come out of hiding, but she didn't want to. Being completely covered by him against these stacks was where she wanted to stay.

"Tristan," her whisper came out even lower, barely audible.

"Nor," he answered.

"Kiss me."

She didn't know where the words came from, but they felt right. And meeting his gaze, she knew he'd do it just the way she wanted.

His hands slowly moved up her body until he was holding her face between them. "Anything for my best friend," he mumbled against her lips.

When he finally closed that tiny bit of space between them, the kiss was slow and sensual, promising and possessive. Thrilling.

When they needed to come up for air, he didn't pull away. They remained as close as can be and Norya lost herself in those perfect green eyes. "You're such a good kisser."

CHAPTER 12
TRISTAN

The storms were crazed outside. The perfect type of weather to shove everyone indoors and make those of them who loved it out there figure out what to do inside.

Norya was one of those outdoorsy people.

Though she'd spent much of the day acquainting herself with the other residents of the palace, helping them with whatever work they had, Tristan knew she'd be heading to his suite soon and he wanted to make sure they met the dusky skies with some fun of their own.

He had the curtains opened fully so they could take in the sky's beauty even with the storm in the way, and all the furniture pushed to the walls to leave the middle empty.

Then he changed out of his everyday wear and finished his preparations with opening the box of symphonies he'd had Evony make him with her magic—a task that required a large payment. One she wouldn't take with coin, but with a favor he wasn't yet sure of. He did know, though, that it would be something annoying and mostly asked to tease him.

When he was finished his preparations, Tristan took a lazy lounge on the couch and watched the door for when Norya presented herself without knocking as was the case daily.

He was lucky to only have to wait a few minutes.

When she entered the common space, letting the door close behind her, she paused and took in the scene. She quirked her brow at the music box, then at Tristan.

She eyed him from head to toe and back up, and that quirked brow rose to question why he was dressed in his formalwear.

"What's all this?" she asked as her fingers found their way through her braid and she let her hair loose.

Tristan loved it like that.

He grinned. "You know a lot, learned a lot while you've been here. But one thing you haven't had a chance to pick up is a formal dance."

She quirked her brow. "A dance?"

He finally rose to meet her on their "dance floor." He held up a hand to invite her to join him, but she didn't move. "You're living here now, Nor. You should learn at least a basic dance. What kind of friend would I be if I didn't teach you?"

"What made you think of this tonight?"

"It's not uncommon for the servants to put together a little festivity in the great hall during a storm. Normally during ones larger than this. I realized earlier that if that were to happen, you'd be lost. And I know if it were to happen, you'd want to join everyone else."

She let her lips tip up. "What makes you think I would? Maybe I'm too above you all."

"Yeah, yeah, yeah, little Islander." He motioned for his hand once more. "Now come."

She didn't fight him as she moved to take his hand. Her

eyes shined as they took in what all this meant. "This is... so soft of you."

He shrugged as he brought her into his arms, placing her hand on his shoulder and securing the other in his. As his free hand settled at the base of her back, he brought her closer. "Just because you're a cold Islander doesn't mean you don't want some softness in your life."

She didn't say anything but by the way her body relaxed into him, trusted him to lead, he knew she was thankful for the effort he'd made tonight.

As Tristan moved her around the room, picking up her stumbling every so often as she stepped in the wrong direction or on his foot, he took in this moment. It wasn't very often that he could get Norya to shut up, to look at him with that awe. It made him want to spend the whole night brainstorming, coming up with more ways to make it happen.

"I... feel like I should change. I showered after helping the others, but I could change into a dres—"

He smirked, pleased she wanted to dress up for him, but teasing all the same. "What dress would you wear exactly?"

She shrugged. "It wasn't very comfortable but I could go get the dress Atiana made for me."

He leaned in close to her. "Don't ever do that."

Her brows furrowed.

"Wear something you're uncomfortable in for me."

Her lips picked up. "You know, behind the assholery, you're a big ole sweetheart."

He kissed her temple, a spot he rarely got to when they were fucking but one he cherished for slower moments. Moments like these which he decided he wanted to make happen more often.

As they moved around the room, Norya's quick learning picking up where to step and how to follow him, Tristan lost himself in the music that played from that box. There weren't many contraptions like that in the North because of the need of a magician, but Tristan had always wanted one. Southerners came out lucky in that regard.

"I'll have a dress made." She broke their silence. "One I actually like. I do like it. Feeling softer sometimes. I don't always want to be the stronger-than-everyone huntress."

"I know," he answered before pulling away to spin her straight back into his arms. "You know, even without a dress, you look beautiful tonight."

She gave a sweet smile. An innocent one. It wasn't one found on the roughened little barbarianette often, but it was captivating.

When the song came to an end, and Tristan slowed their movements, Norya only smiled. When he stepped back to bow to her, she let out a soft giggle. When he stood back up to meet her gaze, she stepped closer and rose to the tips of her toes.

"This is one of my favorite nights now." She kissed that tiny scar on the side of his mouth. "Thank you."

He pushed away from her—which felt completely unnatural—and moved for his final surprise of the night. Sitting on the mantel to his fireplace was a glass bowl filled with sweets.

He moved for her again. "One more, Nor."

The little gasp she made when she looked into the bowl could've kept Tristan happy for the rest of his life. Her grin was shit-eating and her eyes watered—watered!

"You got Gumyons!"

"We were lucky. They came in right before the storm picked up." He couldn't believe she was tearing up.

She snatched the bowl from him and quickly opened a sweet. The moan she let out as her lips closed around the thing was entirely sinful. His cock wanted to make her sound like that.

But instead, Tristan leaned against the wall and watched her enjoy the candy snuggled on the couch as she was. "You're basically a child right now, Nor."

He had no idea what she mumbled around the second piece she'd shoved into her mouth, but he was sure she cussed him in some way. It made him want more of this.

"Yeah, yeah, yeah. Get yourself amped on sugar. We have more dancing to do, then we have some much more fun dancing to do."

Her eyes brightened at the insinuation as she finally placed the bowl aside and moved for the middle of the dance floor.

As he met her there, taking the lead once more, she grinned from ear to ear. "Officially my favorite night ever, Tris."

"Mine too, Nor."

CHAPTER 13

NORYA

The air was especially invigorating after a strong storm. Norya was out in the forests with a couple of hunters, all there for practice and not for the hunt. They had enough in their stores for a few more days, if not another week, and they tried to only kill what they needed.

Norya was in a clearing away from the hunters because as much as she enjoyed their company, being around so many men so often meant she needed her breaks from time to time.

She had her weapons leaning against a tree as she used a throwing star to see if she could cut down an apple that was a little high up on the branch.

"Ah, a weapon you're not already a master in," a voice teased.

Norya caught the star falling back toward her, then turned to see Eddie, one of the other hunters, coming for her. She smiled. "Not for long."

His hands rose for the defensive. "I believe it."

Eddie was in his younger thirties, built, hair shaved down and beard trimmed to perfectly cover his jaw. He was handsome, and Norya hadn't heard any rumors about him, so she was shocked he hadn't yet found his one.

Norya smiled. "Are you out here training as well or were you fooling around with the other hunters? Or were you simply waiting for an opportunity to catch me not proficient in a weapon? Feeling emasculated?"

"How that spy in the Posse keeps you in check is a wonder, woman. You're quite something." He moved closer, hand out for the throwing star as he bit the very tip of his lip, as if he was trying to stop from doing so but unable to help a little nibble.

Norya couldn't blame him. It looked like quite the tasty lip to nibble on. Not quite as much as Tristan's, but...

Maybe she should have a talk with some of the women around the palace grounds, teach them a bit of her Islander ways so one of them could secure a life with Eddie.

She handed the star over and stood back as his wrist flicked beautifully up into the tree, cutting three apples down before he caught the weapon in his hand.

"Lucky me, you chose the one weapon I actually have mastery in."

Norya chuckled. "I've noticed a good amount of you Northerners have a grasp on those things. They're not part of Island culture, like your swords." She bent for an apple and wiped it on her trousers. "Thank you."

His smile was endearing, and Norya knew it'd be easy to find multiple women who may wish for his attentions. She had always enjoyed being an onlooker to claimed couples, even if she'd never wanted to be claimed herself, so it'd be fun to create a claimed couple out of these folk, a project that wasn't quite so rough.

He stepped closer, only about a foot away from brushing her side and slipping behind her so her ass rubbed into his trousers. "Would you like me to teach you?"

Internally, Norya sighed because she knew he was flirting, and maybe in the past she would've taken the bait, but she wasn't feeling up to it. She truly wanted him with one of the palace women, giving said woman a life and future, a family and generations.

She smirked. "What makes you think I wasn't faking my faultiness in order to get attention? What if I'm far better than you?"

"I can only hope so. I'm sure, from all the talk around the palace, that there're many things you could teach me."

All the talk around the palace meant all the gossip about the number of times she and Tristan had been caught. It meant everyone was aware that they were friends-with-benefits, not in a relationship. The thought made her upset.

But why?

She gave a teasing smile. "You need to behave. I can see a future with you and one of the women in the palace."

His grin grew. "I know. Something tells me she's right here."

"Oh yeah? Something?"

"Mhm. Something. Something south of where you're looking now."

Norya's gaze dipped down involuntarily from his eyes to his chest and lower, and she laughed. Cute and funny. And strong from all the times she'd witnessed him hunting while out in the forests.

Before she could say anything more, a voice boomed from toward the palace. "How romantic of a rendezvous."

Tristan was storming toward them, a hard look in his green orbs as he met Eddie's gaze. That one stare told Eddie to get the fuck away before he joined the pile of animals in the storerooms. It was sexy, if unnecessary.

Eddie's hands shot back up. "Hey. We were just having a

friendly chat." Bullshit, but before Norya could say anything, he was off in a hurry. It made her wonder if had she taken him on his offer before Tristan's interruption, if he would've scurried away then too?

She couldn't blame him. Tristan was part of the Posse, and in the North, that truly meant something. With the Master Assassin as a brother and the King as a father figure, Tristan could ruin his life.

But then why would Eddie attempt to flirt if he knew she was fucking Tristan to begin with? In any case, he was probably only horny, and thought her Island upbringing an easier lay. She needed to figure out if he also enjoyed her tougher nature or if the easy lay was his only reason for flirtation in order to know which of the palace women to talk to—the tougher or the softer of the bunch? Something instinctively told her he wanted a softer, more feminine wife, and had simply been horny now. Atiana, the tailor's assistant, came to mind for the softer bunch.

"What's got you so grumpy?" Norya teased Tristan, deciding to think about which woman Eddie might like to claim later.

"Turn around," he ordered instead of answering.

"Excuse me?"

"Turn around. Put your hands on the tree."

When she didn't move, only raised her brows in question, Tristan moved her. He forced her to turn and shoved her hands up to brace herself against the tree, apple forgotten. Then he ripped at the ties to her trousers until they were loose, and he was pulling them down.

When they hit her ankles, his thigh shoved between her legs and made them open as wide as the trousers would allow. He held her still with a grip on her shirt as his opposite hand slithered over the smooth skin of her ass before he smacked her. Hard.

So fucking hard, she winced with the sting.

Then he did so again to the opposite cheek. He was obviously angry with her about something, that hard look in his eyes and his grunts now weren't from their normal rough fucks. These were almost... territorial?

He smacked her again, then shoved his hand between her legs to cup her cunt. "Your pussy's fucking dripping, Nor. Is this because you like when I hit you?" he growled as his fingers slipped through her folds. "Or is this for that fucker?"

Norya breathed hard. "What are you talkin—"

He smacked her again, the sting making her fingernails bite into the tree she was braced against.

"Who're you this wet for, Norya?"

"What the fuck is wrong with you?"

Two fingers shoved into her, curled to hit that spot that he got perfectly. He fucked her hard, letting her moans fill the forests until she was about to come, then pulled away.

"He's not going to fuck you like this," he growled as he pushed his cock inside her, hands on her hips to steady her as he fucked her.

"What"—she clung to the tree—"the fuck"—she gasped at the way his cock hit her and the burn of the bark against her palms—"is wrong with you, spy?"

He didn't answer. His grunts, growls, groans filled the space around them, but he was done talking.

Norya didn't need him to talk anymore. In the moments where she could get her mind to focus past all the pleasure, she realized something Eddie had done had garnered this reaction. What could he have possibly done? He was cute, and made her laugh, and was coming in closer an—

Was her best friend jealous?

She wanted to think on it, but she was already coming, and by the bruising way he held her, he was going to get another orgasm or two out of her before they were done here.

So she let him control her, let him take over her body, faze her mind. She was completely at his mercy.

He smacked her pussy this time, and her orgasm hit without warning, her screams loud enough to carry to the palace greens, to carry to wherever Eddie had run off to.

Tristan bent over to bite down at her ear as he came, his groans sending shivers throughout her body. That sound always made her want more.

When his orgasm subsided, he pulled out and stepped away.

Once Norya could catch her breath, she pushed off the tree and looked at the scratches on her hands. She'd need to make a quick visit to Ashtyn.

As she bent to pull her trousers back up, a pleased groan came from behind her.

She turned as she was tying her trousers to see him waiting for her, a dark look that said he was in no talking mood about his eyes.

She sighed but didn't argue with the look as she grabbed her weapons and they headed for the palace. She didn't know what to think about the possibility that he may have been jealous, may have been claiming her. That wasn't them. They weren't looking to be claimed.

CHAPTER 14
NORYA

Tristan was avoiding one-on-one time with her, but Norya couldn't say she minded. They hadn't been together since the forest two days ago, and he ran away from every opportunity that might leave them alone. She hadn't known what excuse she would use when he asked why she didn't go to his suite at night, but he never asked.

Norya wanted to be annoyed with him for this behavior, but a larger part of her was thankful. She couldn't get it out of her mind that he had fucked her in that forest as a possessive stance, like he was pissing around her to mark her as his property.

The thought itself made her hot, but the meaning behind it made her jittery. Why would he want to possess her? They were friends, best friends after spending every day together for three months, fighting and teasing and being the shoulder the other needed. They'd never complicated their relationship with feelings, and Norya wasn't sure if that was what was happening.

"What's on your mind?" Atiana, the tailor's assistant and the Princess's favorite tailor, brought her out of her thoughts.

She was standing on the podium as Atiana worked another dress on her. This one had trousers under the skirts and a slit that split the skirt in two at the front so it felt more like a cape around her legs than heavy skirts. This was far more to Norya's liking.

Tristan would like it too, though he'd grumble that he still had to peel her trousers off her while she was wearing a dress. She'd have to speak with Atiana about an actual dress later. One she'd love, but also one *he'd* love.

But for now, Atiana's goal was simply about getting Norya to love dresses, and though this technically wasn't one, she couldn't deny she never wanted to take this one off.

Maybe Sael had a point with this girl being the best tailor. She'd been able to read off of simply watching Norya in the other dresses what she would need.

"Everything and nothing at all."

"Are you thinking of Tristan?" Etel, who was normally so quiet, asked. She was Miels's wife, so Norya had no problems believing the two had been speaking of Tristan's and her *different* relationship.

Norya shrugged, in no mood to discuss any of these matters with anyone, least of all these girls.

Evony's head snapped at the mention of the spy. "Did something happen?"

Etel shrugged. "A birdy mentioned they've been avoiding one another."

All eyes snapped to Norya.

She grumbled with all the attention. "Tell your husband to go be a little birdy elsewhere."

Etel's lips twitched up. "You are with his best friend. He cannot help it."

"I am not *with* anyone."

"But you have been avoiding one another?" Sael asked.

Norya shrugged. "He's been avoiding me."

"Why?" Gemma asked. "Did you two have a falling out?"

Norya huffed. "Can the lot of you not mind your business?"

"No," a unanimous calling came from everyone in the room.

Norya rolled her eyes. "The hunters are so much easier to deal with."

"So tell us," Evony started. "Why's our dear brother avoiding you, his most prized fuck?"

Because he'd been territorial the last time he'd fucked her.

Because something about the way Eddie had been with her had pushed him over the edge.

Because something must've been brewing deep down, even if he didn't know of it, that he could no longer fight.

Norya huffed. "I don't know."

"Maybe he needs a break." Ashtyn, who had been dragged —though Norya knew telling her she could try on a few more dresses made doing so easy—by Evony and Gemma, said from her spot pushing through dress after dress on the rack Atiana had brought to her suite from the main tailor's room. "I cannot imagine spending *all* of my time with you lot. It is too much."

"Oh, she's a comedian now," Evony called from her spot on one of the couches.

Ashtyn turned with a wicked grin. "Seriously though. Maybe he has a lot on his mind about where they stand and he needs time to think about it."

Atiana eyed her through the mirror as she completed the finishing pieces to Norya's dress. "Is that so?"

Something about Atiana's demeanor made speaking with her the simplest of things. "It may be so."

"What could he have to think about?" Evony asked.

"Do you think he is finally growing feelings?" Gemma added.

"Who's to say he didn't have feelings from the beginning," Sael voiced. "Maybe he's simply tired of holding it in now."

"Maybe it's that..."

Norya stopped listening to them. It did not matter what they thought. It only mattered what she knew.

And she knew feelings were growing, sprouting out of places they'd both tried desperately to suppress. Was that why she hadn't considered sleeping with Eddie? Why the entire time she thought about who he could be with instead?

It couldn't be. She was sure it was simply because she enjoyed seeing how claimed couples came to be and how they grew together—though as she spent time with Atiana, something instinctive told her Eddie wouldn't be for her. She'd have to find another soft woman for him. It'd be a nice distraction from the mess in her head. Because her biggest, and scariest, question still stood unanswered—did she hold feelings for Tristan now, past being best friends?

Norya desperately hoped the answer was negative.

It wasn't negative.

One look at him as he opened the door to his suite proved as much. A negative answer to whether or not she was growing feelings for him would mean she wouldn't have a reaction to seeing him. A negative definitely wouldn't have her heart racing at the sight of him, looking as delicious as ever but also looking like...

Hers?

He looked defeated as he stepped aside to let her in, then closed the door behind her.

"You've been avoiding me," she opened, needing to get this out in the open.

"Have I?"

"Haven't you?"

He shrugged. "Possibly."

"Why? What changed in the forest?"

He shook his head. "Nothing. I... don't know. Nothing."

"I know."

He quirked a brow as he sat on the arm of his couch.

"Killian acted like that with Sael. Men act like that when they claim their woman."

He scoffed. "You've got to be kidding me."

"You Northerners are more reserved, but if you've grown feelings, why hide them? Why suffer holding them in?"

"I wouldn't know."

"I hadn't realized it, Tris. Not before a couple of days ago." She stood in the middle of the room, unsure how things got to this point. "You were claiming me. In that moment, even though there was no one around to see us, you were claiming me."

Was she really going to do this? Was seeing him now, knowing the answer wasn't negative really going to push her to the edge?

It had to. She was an Islander. They didn't push around their thoughts. She was raised to always speak her mind, to not allow anything to dwindle and fester in her.

"I was doing no su—"

"I hadn't realized until that moment that maybe there were feelings between us. Or maybe the feelings were so new, there was no way I could've known any earlier."

"I don't have fee—"

"I've realized that you're my best friend. But more so than before. Before, I thought we were as close as you and Miels."

"We ar—"

"But I've realized it's more like Miels and Etel. Sparrow and Evony. Killian and Sael. James and Gemma."

"Norya, we're not toget—"

"I think I've fallen for you. Or I'm falling for you. I don't know. How do you tell when you're on the journey or arrived at the destination?"

He started to stand. "You're being ridiculous. You don't have feel—"

"You know I cannot stand living in half-truths, Tristan. You're more than a fuck buddy now, and I cannot stand the thought of anyone else touching you."

When did that happen? She only realized a few minutes ago that she had feelings for him at all. When did that jump from feelings to possession to claiming?

"Don't say that. Don't start making declarations."

"Why not? It's the truth."

Somehow, even if she hadn't realized it until the words were out, it was the truth.

"I was never looking for a wife, Nor. You knew that. You were never going to be my wife, my claimed woman, any of it."

"And I wasn't looking for a male, but I cannot help this fee—"

"No! Stop it. That's not us," he argued.

"There's no other us, Tristan. I cannot think of you without my heart skipping now." When did that start to happen? How fast was her heart racing now? "I cannot look at you without hoping you'll take my hand or hug me or lean in to tell me I'm beautiful." Since when did she want those softer moments she saw in couples? "I cannot bear to be around you without knowing with certainty that I'm yours and you're mine." Was this what it truly meant to be claimed?

"There is no loving future for me, Nor. We were clear about that."

"Yeah, well, the lines are blurred now, Tris."

"And I'm remaining on my side."

She scoffed. "You know you were marking your property when you took me. You know the thought of me with another male makes you sick. You know you don't want me with anot—"

"Be with another male!" he roared. "You are not my claim. You are not my wife. *We* were clear on those matters. You were nothing but a fuck, Nor."

She grit her jaw as she subconsciously stepped back. "Fine. But I'm going to need time. To get rid of this festering." Was that possible? "You've avoided me for two days. Keep it up. There is no reason for us to be around one another past Posse matters."

She didn't wait around for him to respond. She simply turned and calmly walked out.

She made her way to the suite she shared with the nonas, and tried to remain calm as she made her way past them by the corner table and into her room. She wasn't sure if they truly didn't notice how tense she was or if they knew not to question her at the moment, but Norya was left alone.

She huffed angrily as she lay in bed. What the fuck was going on with her? She needed these flutterings in her chest to go away. How the fuck did she *fall* for Tristan?

Ugh, she wanted to punch until her hands fell off, but instead she turned in bed and fell asleep. The fucking ass didn't deserve another moment of her thoughts.

CHAPTER 15

TRISTAN

He couldn't take the things she said out of his mind.

Why would she believe he'd been claiming her? Why would she think he wanted any more than the relationship they already had? What had it been that made her believe his feelings were now involved?

His heart hurt. Not because of any ridiculous feelings he might have, but at the fact that he'd hurt his best friend, his favorite person. Because that's what she'd become—the person he cherished above all else. The very last thing he ever wanted to do was hurt her.

But he couldn't figure out what had possessed her to come to his suite the night before and make them, what? Official?

"We're going to need first-hand account about this plague." Miels's voice brought Tristan from his thoughts.

He was thankful for this meeting. He could finally get the mess his friendship had become out of his mind, and hopefully before the men figured something was wrong and wanted to walk about it. Only a few months ago, Tristan would have come out with the problem immediately, getting their opinions on the matter, but not anymore. Not when they had women they liked to blab to, women who would harass Tristan once they knew.

"Based on the probabilities of the historical sicknesses we've been comparing to, we think we've figured out what healers have been able to heal in the past and what they haven't been able to. Any physical aspects that are making it so —like a poultice someone is making—a healer would easily be able to take care of. Something they are ingesting, if it is something that has been added to their bloodstream. If any of those check out, Ashtyn will be needed, and the process to finding out if *she* can heal them, and therefore meaning there might be another Master in this palace will begin," he added.

"What is the alternative if not those?" James asked.

Tristan answered this time to keep his mind busy from wavering back to his little barbarianette. "Something like the poison that was set near the palace a few months ago. Something airborne would require a magician." Sparrow stiffened, readying to deny allowing Evony to help when Tristan added, "But with Evony's pregnancy, we don't want her expending so much so it might then require more magicians to come together to clear it. It could then be a healthy introduction of magicians to Northerners and finally break this long-held disapproval of them in the North. Magicians will slowly go back to being allowed into these lands."

"That would make Ed's job easier," Sparrow answered.

King Edmund had spent much of his time slowly rolling out the goodness of magicians, but nothing would help more than magicians saving Northern lives.

"It might come down to needing both," James answered. "We might still need to incorporate magicians from the South."

Sparrow nodded. "We can head ou—"

"No," Tristan interrupted. "Your wife is pregnant. You won't be leaving her side. As is your wife," Tristan added before James could volunteer.

"Tris and I can handle this on our own," Miels added, not bothering to add Killian, who was currently out with the hunters, into their mix since he tried to stay away from the politics of the palace. Fat chance considering marrying the Princess made him future King.

"All right," Sparrow surprisingly didn't argue. "I'll inform Ed two of us will be remaining. He was probably ready to throw a party with us all gone."

Tristan scoffed to hide his laugh. "Right. He would've probably given you anything to stay. Leaving him alone with all the women, two of them hormonal from pregnancy—he was probably ready to volunteer to join us."

They all laughed.

THEY WERE IN THE STABLES, Gabriel having prepared their horses already. Evony and Gemma had come out to say their goodbyes even though the trip would take all of three days.

Sparrow and James had rolled their eyes at the ways their wives had clung to him and Miels, then been all too happy to take them back to their suites. Ro stayed by Killian's side, but she smiled and waved at them as a thank-you for protecting this nation and its people. She was going to make an amazing queen one day.

Norya stood beside her brother by the stairs. She didn't come down to say bye, and Tristan wasn't sure how to feel about it.

That was a fucking lie.

He hated it. She was his best friend. Not having her tight ass fucking hugs before he left, unable to touch her for days, was torture. It also stung knowing he'd promised to take her to see more of the North, yet she wouldn't even come near him now to say bye. Was this the new them? Was she going to stay away indefinitely? She couldn't have feelings for him. The thought was preposterous.

He wanted her to come up and wish him a safe journey because even though it was unlikely, he *could* get hurt while out. It could be their final conversation had. It was why the others did it, no matter how short the journey may be. And the very last thing Tristan wanted was for their last conversation to be about how he didn't want her. The last thing he wanted was for his last words to her to be 'You were nothing but a fuck, Nor.' She was so much more than just a fuck.

But she had asked him one simple favor—to stay away—and that was what he'd do.

With Edmund and the nonas having been the first to wish them a well journey, Etel was the final one left. She gave Tristan a hug and kiss on the cheek, so sweet and small in his arms before she moved for her husband. They embraced and kissed, and because they were standing close enough to Tristan, he heard them mumble to one another.

"I hate that you keep leaving me," Etel muttered against his lips.

"Fall pregnant, and I'll be stuck by your side." Miels smirked.

The comment almost made Tristan burst out laughing. Miels had been trying to get Etel pregnant since they got married, but she was too smart to rely on the anti-pregnancy concoctions *he* made. She knew he would be throwing in placebos instead.

"You keep leaving me, and we won't have an opportunity to fall pregnant," the little thing teased.

Miels laughed as he kissed the tip of her nose. "I'll make coming home worth it, little creature."

"I love you, big creature," she mumbled.

"I love you more," he responded.

"I know," she teased again, getting a rough kiss and a smack on the ass from the spy.

Etel turned red as she walked away. The poor thing was definitely not used to these public displays. As a Northerner, Tristan couldn't entirely blame her. Even if he and Norya had been caught a few too many times in their private moments, they still weren't publicly touchy. Tristan was surprised Norya fit into that part of the Northern custom easily.

Miels turned to the horses he and Tristan would be taking. "Are you saying bye to Nor?"

Tristan got on his horse. "I waved."

Miels quirked a brow. "That's it?"

"What else is needed? We'll be back in a few days."

"But she's your—"

"She's not my anything. We were friends who fucked. That's it. If she doesn't wish to come up to say her farewells, she certainly doesn't have to."

Miels whistled as they turned their horses to be on their way. "We'll be talking about this on the ride."

Fucking great.

CHAPTER 16

TRISTAN

Miels tried to get him to talk the entire ride out to the middle of the Northern Lands. When it didn't work, he insisted he would come back to the matter, and began instead speaking of his wife pregnant. The googly way he spoke of her almost made Tristan break his silence on Norya only to get him to shut up. And he was almost certain that hadn't been Miels's plan. The man was simply smitten.

They were in Aldridge where they'd heard of a decent amount of sick, but not as much as some of these other villages. Hopefully this meant he and Miels could stay healthy around them. They were running a risk being there, the possibility of taking the plague into the palace a large one, but the fact that it wasn't contagious soothed some of their nerves. Though to be safe, they'd also brought their own food and drinking water to make sure they didn't take in anything in the villages. If it was something there making them sick rather than someone, then they needed to be cautious.

With the horses tied to trees at the edge of the village, he and Miels moved for the hut where Marcanz, the little shop's owner, lived in the back. He was their confidant when they were in Aldridge because he loved his people and wanted the palace's help in any way. Even without a plague, he always helped Tristan and Miels in the hopes that they could get updated utilities or different wagons of food or something exciting for their less lucrative village.

Marcanz was seated behind a table where he waited for customers to make their purchases, and sat straight up at the sight of them. There was a hopeful smile on his face—one he normally didn't wear, even when the thought of a prize for his village was exciting. "Are you here for the sick?"

Tristan caught his brother's eye. It must've been quite something if he was so hopefully they'd have a cure for it. "We are. For research only at the moment."

Marcanz's head moved in fast nods as he quickly ran for the entrance to his shop, turning the sign to closed, then guided them with the same speed to the door behind his table that led to his living quarters. "Come. Come. As I'm sure you've heard. It isn't contagious."

He normally wasn't so secretive, merely waiting for customers to leave the shop in order to talk to them. He'd certainly never closed down his shop and insisted they go back to his living quarters.

Neither he nor Miels said a word as they followed the man to the back.

It was a quaint space, but lovely. There was a small kitchenette in the corner, a door that led to the bathing chamber beside the door they'd just walked in from, and a small table on the other side. In the final corner was a foldable wall put in place to give the semblance of privacy. Tristan knew many people used them to make one room feel like two, to make their bedroom feel like its own space.

As Tristan moved to ask why they were back there, a cough that sounded more like a croaking cry for help came from behind that makeshift wall.

Marcanz was already in his kitchenette, readying a boiling pot of water for tea. He gave them a sad smile before raising his voice for the sick behind the divider. "Honey, we have company. It is T and M from the palace. Remember I told you they come by from time to time to learn of the goings on."

Another cough racked the space before her feeble voice was heard. "Why are they here? Don't they have a rebellion to handle? That's far more important than a little sickness."

Marcanz was visibly upset, and Tristan couldn't blame him. Even if his wife was right. A rebellion would be more important. It was why, atop hoping this was the common sickness, they'd focused on it rather than the plague for majority of the year. "The rebellion is taken care of. We are preparing for the plague now, but we need more information to be prepared when our healer starts her job."

The older man prepared four cups of tea, dousing the one for his wife with honey and lemon, then nodded for the back. "You do not have to sit so close to her, but come."

They'd wanted to see some of the sick, so this worked perfectly.

Tristan and Miels sat on chairs at the end of the little space, backs to the divider. In this makeshift bedroom was their bed, these two chairs, and a side table. They didn't have an excess of anything, and Tristan knew it was because Marcanz always insisted they didn't need much else, so they would help the community instead of keeping the money.

"If you do not mind," Miels started after Marcanz handed everyone their teas. "Can you tell us when you realized you'd fallen with the plague?"

"The first time was when I visited the neighboring town, Baysoven," she said with her rough voice.

"First time?" Tristan asked.

"We thought we had cured her, but less than two weeks later, she was sick again. And she hadn't gone to the town, so it wasn't because of that."

"Can you let us know what the symptoms were that led you here? We've heard people aren't getting symptoms much. They just have a sudden change to their body?" Miels asked.

Marcanz took over since his wife's throat hurt too much to continue talking. "Suddenly. It is how we knew it had to be this plague. That is how everyone has gone down. Fine one moment, then coughing up a storm the next until they fall. Then they're laid up in bed, sweating and freezing. We are lucky—Annie's vomiting has not been so much, but not all are so. I've heard of a few people around town who haven't been able to stop. Then there are those who are spitting up blood. They are completely dehydrating their bodies."

"You said you got better, then sick again. Does it feel the same both times?"

Annie shook her head. "It's drained more of me this time. I feel weaker, less able to fight this attack on my body."

"Have any died in your village?" Tristan asked. He knew it would be a sensitive subject, especially given how sick Annie was, but he needed to know.

Marcanz's entire face shifted, even more upset now. "Two. One of them only a nine-year-old boy. They are both from the east of our village."

"If you do not mind, Marcanz, after you inform us of how the sickness has affected your Annie, would you show us to the family of the dead? I suspect if theirs died, it can be because they had more exposure to whatever has caused this." Because it was clear it wasn't contagious. If Marcanz had been taking care of Annie all this time and not caught it, it must not have been an airborne problem.

The Posse had suspected as much, but they needed to be sure. This made Ashtyn a more possible healer. If it was airborne, getting her to heal the air would've been nearly impossible. Magicians would be the only hope then. Emphasis on hope.

"Of course," Marcanz answered as he took his wife's hand. "My Annie has a pounding vein in her leg that has become visible." He moved the comforter over to show her bare legs, the left one with a dark vein slithering from ankle to right above the knee. "Her voice is changing because of how violent the coughs are, so she tries not to talk so much to keep herself at bay. It seems to be working for now. She..."

Marcanz went on, all the while holding poor little Annie's hand. Tristan placed his still full cup of tea on the ground—sticking to the plan of not ingesting anything they didn't bring themselves—and paid close attention. As awful as it was for Marcanz and Annie to go through this, Tristan saw the love between them.

He couldn't imagine anyone he loved like this. He couldn't imagine any of his Posse like this, couldn't imagine his best friend lying in bed and being able to only sit beside her. He could only imagine Marcanz wanted to take Annie's spot. It's what he'd do if Norya ever fell sick like this.

CHAPTER 17

NORYA

Etel was a sweet girl, shy and small and always with a little lift to her lips. She was very Northern, so when she asked Norya for lessons with the bow and arrow, it'd certainly been a shock. Not as much so when Norya learned the girl had taken down a grown rebel and had been training herself with a sandbag in her room for a long time before Miels became part of the picture.

Since then, Miels had been giving her trainings to make sure she could handle hand-to-hand, apparently deciding as the men of the Posse that they would no longer shelter their women since it definitely hadn't worked out in Sael's favor.

But still, she didn't know weapons.

"How exactly is this supposed to remain a secret from your husband?" Norya asked the girl as they stopped in a clearing in the forest only a few yards from the palace greens. "Even if the whole palace agrees not to speak a word, he's obsessed with you. He'll track you down and find out everything there is to know."

She laughed. "I know. Which is why it's going to be a

surprise for when he comes back in a couple of days. Then he'll insist on helping teach me weapons as well."

Norya smirked. "Pick up the bow and arrow, and string it before you replace me altogether."

They'd just gone over how to do so, so although her arms struggled the entire time, Etel was able to do so. She inhaled to steady her breathing as the weapon aimed at a tree across the clearing. "Miels isn't amazing with the bow and arrow. I'll allow you to keep your job if you're good at it."

Norya laughed. "Wow. Being a Posse member really changed you, huh?"

She was joking. Clearly given she'd only known Etel as a Posse member, but there was a slight change to her now than when Norya first met the girl three months ago. Then, she was more quiet and stuck to her husband's side. Now, she explored more.

Norya knew it was because she was finally becoming more comfortable with the idea of being part of the Posse.

"As it's changing you," Etel answered. "Always for the better."

"I am not part of the Posse. My brother is," Norya answered before commanding, "Release the arrow. Let's see what we're starting with."

Etel's lips twitched up, and Norya was reminded immediately of her husband. The two spent so much time together, they were beginning to act like one another—Miels with all the remedies he spoke of, and Etel with his cocky behaviour.

When the arrow went flying, it skimmed straight past the tree and landed on the ground a few yards out.

"Wow," Norya sounded. "You actually almost got it. Are you sure this is your first time with the weapon?"

Etel nodded. "After learning how to kinda fight based

solely off watching Miels, I realized I was picking up other things too. I've liked watching you too."

"That's kinda sexy."

The girl blushed as her gaze flew downward, and a mumble left her. "Thank you."

Northerners amused her. They had their moments where they could be so normal—at least, Norya's version of normal—then they'd go back to their propriety. She wondered if she'd ever grow accustomed to it.

Norya tapped on the girl's nose to get her attention once more. "Don't be too thankful, dear little Etel. We don't want Miels getting jealous of *us*, do we?"

The way she said us insinuated a lot, and Norya was sure the expert picked it up by the way she reddened.

"I'm sure both he and Tristan would enjoy the show," Etel muttered instead. "In theory. In actuality, he would rip your hands off for touching me."

"Yes," Norya conceded. "And Tristan would never watch you. Being Miels's means you're his little sister. That would be disturbing. But in theory, they'd love it, they'd absolutely love to say they love it at least."

As they laughed, Norya raised the weapons in Etel's hands once more. "Now, back to these lessons."

"You're the one who started talking of others," she muttered, then even lower, "Of Tristan."

"What did you say, tiny little expert?"

Those blushing cheeks reminded Norya of when Sael was on the Island. She'd constantly been blushing. Still did, but those first few weeks had been a deeper crimson.

"Nothing." When she caught Norya's quirked brow and the fact that they weren't continuing until she spoke up, Etel sighed. "Just. I know you two have been staying away from one another, and I know after months together, it must be killing you. I figure it is because you have realized your feelings?"

"You figure, or your husband figures?"

Etel's smile broadened. "We figured. Tristan's more closed on the matter than you are, so I'm bringing in more of the evidence at the moment."

Norya shook her head as she went back to Etel's weapons. "You guys gossip too much," she mumbled before beginning to boss the expert around.

The bossing around lasted a little over half an hour before the small thing's arms were shaking as she tried to lift the bow and pull the arrow. Right as Norya was about to call it for the day, they were interrupted. "You've done an amazing job, Etel."

Atiana was standing behind them, silently observing.

"How long have you been there?" There was no way Norya hadn't sensed her this entire time.

"Only the last shot. It was well done. I predict that is your compliment to take?"

Norya shrugged. "It is both of ours."

Atiana smiled. "Would either of you mind, then, if next time I join you?"

Etel's hands landed together as she giddily smiled. "That'd be lovely. I didn't know you wanted to learn too?"

She shrugged. "There're a lot of things I've wanted to learn that I haven't had the confidence to do in all these years. I think I will change that now. You girls are showing me as much."

Norya couldn't believe someone as beautiful as her hadn't had the confidence to ask for certain lessons. She'd heard the men within the palace—hunters, guards, medics, cooks, all of them—speak of the things they'd like to do to her. As the most beautiful female at the palace, she'd have a line of men willing to help if she ever gave them the time of day.

"I'd be happy to teach you as well. As many of you as I could turn into Islanders, the better."

They both laughed as Etel said, "I highly doubt we'll become barbarians because we can wield a weapon."

Norya quirked a teasing brow at her. "Turning right into your husband."

All three laughed, and Norya took a second to enjoy this—time with women. It was something she was so unaccustomed to having since she had to fend for herself her entire life. She grew up more barbarian than barbarianette, so she'd never gotten very close with the females on the Island. It'd always been the thing to sadden her most, but she'd figured it was a small case in all the larger problems life could throw at her.

Finding females—both Etel and Atiana, and those other women in the Posse—wasn't something Norya had been expecting in coming to the North—especially with their propriety—but she found she loved it. Especially when Gemma and Evony's lack of propriety was thrown into the mix.

"I will prepare myself garms tonight, then I should be ready whenever you two decide to come back out."

It was quite cold in the middle of autumn, so the special garms were more a requirement than not. Not that they couldn't go without, but it was better if they were comfortably warm so they could focus on the lesson and not their body's shivers.

As they all headed back for the palace, Atiana's gaze wandered up. "You think there's a storm coming?"

"Absolutely," Etel answered. "Hopefully it waits for our boys to get home first."

Yes. Hopefully. The thought of anything happening to those boys felt like an arrow piercing straight through Norya's chest.

She sighed. Caring for people was more trouble than she would've ever given credit to.

CHAPTER 18
TRISTAN

"You sure you want to do this?" Miels followed him toward the tavern.

"You've never asked me that question before. Why would I not be sure?"

Miels stopped him with a hand on the shoulder before Tristan could head inside. "Because, like me, you have a female at home who would be upset by the fact. Heartbroken."

"What is your problem with calling her my female? We are not together. I do not feel for her what you do for Etel, mate. We fuck. It's absolutely amazing, and I'd love to enjoy it forever, but without the feelings. I don't want any of that, so stop trying to force it on me."

"I'm not forcing anything on you, mate. I know you're into her. She brings out a side of you that plays along the edge. That's a side you hardly share, even with Spar and me."

"So that means I must be in love with her? Can it not be that she's simply a closer friend than you or Spar?"

"Clearly, considering I'd never let you fuck me," Miels muttered, causing a grin Tristan tried to force down. "But you know she's yours. Think of her with another male, and tell me she is not."

Why did everyone want him to think of Norya with another male? He didn't want to. That wasn't his kink.

"You cannot. The same way the thought of you with another female will kill her. Don't do this because you're afraid to have feelings for her."

"Let her be with another male. Why would it bother me that my best friend is getting pleased?" He grimaced at his own words.

Miels smirked. "Really? You're going to act like you'd be okay with another male kissing her, touching her, sticking his cock in her?"

His body twitched with the need to hit something, but Tristan forced himself to calm. "It is her body. She can do with it as she likes."

"Well, apparently she likes what you have to give. In that case, I know a couple of guys at the palace that are similar to us. I'll send them over to her when we get home."

"I'm done talking about this." Tristan shoved away.

He had his back to his friend but still heard, "I'll be in our room. Hopefully you join me rather than some whore."

It felt calming to step into the tavern and leave the drama his friend was trying to create outdoors, but not as much as he'd hoped. Coming to the taverns had always been a fun occasion, and though less so by himself, Tristan was determined to have as good a time as any in the past, without the images Miels had just created plaguing his thoughts.

A majority of Northerners chose to stay away from alcohol, so while Tristan did catch a couple people with the inebriating drinks, most had waters or sparkling drinks in hand. Tristan chugged down the large cup of water he'd brought with him to entirely clear his head, then turned with a grin he had to force onto his face. He was determined to have a good time.

The moment he turned, his gaze latched on to a plump red-headed woman who was eyeing him like a creature its prey. His lips tore up into a wicked grin as he moved for her, water from his drink still dripping down his jaw.

He leaned in close once he was beside her. "Be careful sitting here all alone. There're a sinful amount of things that could be done to that body."

She giggled as a finger took some of the water from his chin. She licked the digit clean, and Tristan smirked as he followed the movement. As he watched her suck her own finger back, then followed those lips up to the hazel eyes of... some random woman.

Tristan cleared his throat and shook out of his thoughts. Of course it would be a random woman. Who else was he expecting?

That finger slipped from her mouth to trail up the arm he had resting on the table. "What exactly would you do?" she cooed seductively. "I'm taking notes. Trying to see who would do my body best."

Tristan bit his bottom lip. She was a tease. He liked that. They were always more fun when they wanted to build the tension first rather than simply jump on one another.

Tristan flipped their hands quickly, so he held her wrist down. "All you need to know is that I'd be in charge."

Though her eyes were glimmering, she winced and pulled at her arm a little. It broke Tristan from the haze. She liked him in control, but wasn't able to handle what he wanted to give her. It wasn't something Tristan had ever realized in all of the women he'd had before. He'd never been so rough as he was now.

He wanted to be rough. He didn't have soft moments

because those meant there was a relationship to cherish. He'd have to get over how rough he wanted it though, and behave himself—hard but softer than what he'd become accustomed to these past three months.

Her legs spread, each ankle wrapping around his waist to bring him closer while her free hand slithered up his chest. "I can't wait to see what you'd do to my body." Her legs shoved him closer, hand slipped higher on his chest. "How wet do you want me before we begin, baby."

The memory of nails scraping up his thighs, down his back, over his chest, each leaving angry pink marks.

Teeth marks marring his thighs, neck, back, each placed when he wouldn't stop moving.

Dark tangles of hair falling over every inch of his skin as her mouth hovered over him.

All of it was a distraction.

Her fingers running down his chest as dark-brown orbs looked up at him through long eyelashes. The way she always smirked, telling him without words that he was hers to do as she pleased.

"The lines are blurred now, Tris."

This would kill her.

He didn't need to have feelings for her to know this would kill her.

He didn't need to have feelings for her to know this would kill him.

Tears trailing down the face of the strongest woman he'd ever known. Fists clenching as she tried to act like it didn't matter. Body racking as she cried herself to sleep because the man she'd fallen for, her best friend, was off fucking some random whore.

He couldn't do this.

Not only because it would hurt his best friend, but because

it'd be unfair to this woman. He'd spend the entire night thinking of Norya, wishing it were her he was licking and fucking.

Tristan pushed away from the redhead quickly, shocking her.

"What's wrong?" she exclaimed.

He shook his head and walked off. "I can't do this."

He was out of the tavern quickly, breathing in the night air. He may not be in love with her the way everyone wanted him to be, but he still loved her. She'd taken Miels's spot as his best friend, and he couldn't bear being the reason she was so hurt.

Even knowing not reciprocating those feelings was hurting her.

He would go back to whoring, but he would do as she asked first, and allow those feelings to go away. He could do at least that much for his best friend.

He took deep lungfuls before making his way to the inn room he was sharing with Miels—the last one available.

When he got to the room, he stripped out of his shoes and shirt and joined Miels in the bed.

He didn't have to see his brother to know he was awake, waiting for him, and there was now a wide smirk on the ass's face.

"Glad you made the right decision, mate."

"Whatever. Go to sleep."

CHAPTER 19
NORYA

"Aw," Nona Tereza's teasing voice caught Norya. "There's our dear girl, not hiding from us for a change."

"I could rectify that rather quickly if you'd like." Norya gave a sickly sweet smile as she joined them at the table in the corner of their suite.

Nona Tereza's eyes narrowed as Nona Eleni's sparked with amusement. "Behave, dear, or I'll kick you out of this suite." She scoffed at herself before Norya could say anything. "What good that would do. You would simply jump into Tristan's bed, and be much happier there anyway."

Norya played with the strings the nonas were knitting with, a bowl of raisins sitting in the middle of the table for their snacking pleasure. "I wouldn't do that."

She'd probably go to Etel's workstation and sleep in the room the expert had back there, the one she hadn't used since moving in with Miels.

Or over to Atiana where she could be in a nice room and have someone outside their group to talk to. The girl was such a good listener, and though normally spoke little, she always did so with calm truth.

"Whyever not?" Nona Tereza asked. "You've happily spent nearly every night there since we arrived to the North."

"Maybe that's the problem. He isn't mine. I shouldn't be spending all my time with him."

Both nonas gave her the look that said she wasn't going anywhere until they got their answers. Not that she had any plans of running away.

"What's brought that way of thinking on?" Tereza asked.

She shrugged, sighed, and paid close attention to the way her hands played with the yarn. "It's kinda ridiculous, no? I spend as much time with him during the day as any of the couples in the Posse. I spend my nights in his bed like the others spend together. We are only friends. I've set myself up for failure by acting exactly as the others have, and I hadn't even realized it until now."

"And is there a reason you've realized it now?" Tereza asked.

Because I confessed my feelings for him, and he shot me down. Because I realized I have feelings for him. Because I'm still not absolutely certain that claiming is something I want because damn, does it suck to give someone else this much control of my life.

"Can I lie?"

A hand landed on hers, rubbing it soothingly. "Sure, dear."

"I've decided to stay away so I don't grow feelings for him. So it doesn't get to a point where I confess my feelings, and he shuts them down. So we don't have to get to a point where I tell him to stay away from me so I can get over my feelings. He's my best friend, and I'd hate not to spend time with him every day."

Another hand landed on her forearm, thumb running soft circles. "Sometimes men need a push, Norya mi loria."

Norya's lips twitched up without permission. 'Mi loria' was what Nona Eleni used to call her when she was first becoming part of their family. She said the plant Loria was used to weave crowns, and Norya was a goddess, a queen the way she fended for herself, so it was the only name that would make sense with her.

"Or sometimes," Tereza added in a more somber tone, "it is simply not meant to be, and you move on. You decided which you believe it to be now?"

She glanced up at them. "You two know which it is, don't you?"

They both smiled, and Eleni answered, "We would only rob you of the chance to experience and grow from what you've learned if we tell you. You're amazing at a great many things, mi loria, but feelings have never been your strong suit. I think you need this lesson."

Norya scoffed. "I think I need a bath."

Both nonas laughed as Tereza added, "Don't think on it too much, deary. Allow things to happen as they will, and you'll be quite happy with the results."

She couldn't imagine being happy with anything but snuggling up with Tristan to sleep, but she listened to them and tried to push him out of her thoughts. There were so many other things to think of and so many other guys at the palace, that it shouldn't be too difficult.

BEFORE HEADING TO THE BATH, Norya stopped by the cottage to the side of the palace where the stablehand lived. Gabriel opened the door topless, giving Norya a very nice view as she followed him inside. She internally laughed at the thought of Ashtyn ripping her head off for this little rendezvous.

"Wow, I must have the best luck imaginable."

His lips tipped up as he moved in and she followed. "How's that?"

"I keep coming to you half naked. It's a gift to women, stablehand."

He laughed as he disappeared into his room. "Thank you."

As Norya waited out in the common area, she found herself at his table, picking at the woodworking he was currently working on. There were shavings all over the table and the knife he used for the work beside the piece of wood.

It was a bird of some sort. Beautiful.

Norya wasn't even aware she was picking it up until it was in her hand. Then she couldn't help but traced the details. It wasn't yet done, but it was still so detailed. She couldn't imagine the amount of patience and love that went into work like this. No wonder Gabriel was willing to wait for Ashtyn as long as it took.

"It's one of the cattle egrets." His voice right behind her scared Norya. "They hang around the horse to help get ticks and insects off them. Sometimes, I like carving them and handing them out to the kids in town."

She placed it back down. "You're sweet."

He gave that handsome smile. "So I've been told." He raised his hand, showing her the leather piece she was there for. "Your pouch. It should easily strap on to your horse and you can keep your arrows safely secured in here"—he showed her the large opening and the clasp that kept it closed—"and hang about two bows from from"—he showed a strap that was easily accessible—"and if you wanted, you could even take it off the horse and carry it on your shoulder with this strap."

"Wow, Gabriel. I think that's your word. Wow."

He laughed as he handed it over. "I'm glad you like it."

"What do I owe you for it?"

"Nothing. I do not need money."

"Then a favor."

"I don't need that either. It is a gift. From one friend to another."

She smiled. He may not ask for anything, but Norya knew of one thing he'd always want—Ashtyn's safety. And with the healer's travels coming soon—ones Norya was going to be on, whether Tristan liked it or not—she knew that was the best gift she could give him.

"Thank you, Gabriel." She kissed his cheek and left for the night.

Ashtyn really was stupid. How she could have that perfect specimen of a man and deny him was incredible.

Incredibly stupid, that is.

AT THE PALACE BATHS, Norya realized she'd been wrong.

It was difficult not to think of her best friend.

It was like Tristan was playing games with her mind. Every time she truly began to get distracted—thinking of hunting or Etel's lessons coming up or the way Atiana wanted to make her a nicer set of trouser and vest or the rooms she liked to explore in the palace—Tristan would pop back into her mind, always wanting to be part of the experience.

The memory of his hand on her pussy while they were hunting.

The smirk he'd wear watching her boss Etel around, telling her he loved when she was bossy like that. That night, she would be in control of their fuck.

The way he'd eye her in a nicer set of clothes, kiss her cheeks and joke that she was turning into a girl. He knew how much she cherished time with the other women and how much she wanted to be more like them.

The chase he'd give to find the most exciting parts of the palace to explore together, trying to keep their hands off each other once they got to a spot that was too remote for servants to be casually passing by.

Everything she did had an ounce of him in it.

So she'd tried thinking of other men.

Because there was no way he would join her then.

But that didn't last either.

Any time she thought of a guard, servant, hunter, anyone who she may fancy—even for a simple fuck—Tristan's angry face popped into her mind telling her she wasn't allowed to be touched by anyone but him. Which was absolutely ridiculous considering he had quite literally told her he didn't care if she was with other males.

So the bath wasn't quite as relaxing as she'd hoped, but in those moments where Tristan was forgotten, she'd truly enjoyed herself.

Now changed and back to her suite, she wasn't quite ready for a quiet night where her thoughts would be far too loud.

So when she walked into her suite to find the nonas nowhere to be found, and all the girls inside, she wasn't sure if she was happy or upset. On the one hand, they'd make it so loud, she wouldn't have a chance to be in her thoughts.

And on the other, they'd want to speak of Tristan.

"What're you lot doing in here?" she asked as she closed the door behind herself.

The four girls from the Posse were there along with the grumpy healer and the beautiful tailor.

"Keeping you company," Sael answered as she smacked a pillow beside herself on the ground for Norya to sit on.

As Norya took her spot, she eyed the others, most sitting on the ground as well, with the exception of Ashtyn who was lying on the couch. "Why?"

"We heard you may need a distraction for the night, so no speaking of he-who-must-not-be-named," Gemma teased. "We all have our own complaints about our men. It'd be nice to spend the night letting those off our shoulders."

"Yes!" Evony exclaimed. "You be the judge. Are we being crazy or are our men?"

Norya eyed both women's bellies. Pregnancy hormones meant they were probably the crazy ones, but she wasn't going to tell them that. Then she eyed the others. "Are Ashtyn and Atiana also judges?"

"Atiana yes," Evony answered.

"Ashtyn no," Gemma finished.

"Why not?" the healer exclaimed.

"You have a man," they answered together.

"No I don't! Norya has more of a man than I do."

"False," Gemma pointed out, then completely ignored her, making everyone giggle, as she turned to Norya, then Atiana. "James has decided that..."

CHAPTER 20

TRISTAN

Miels was annoyingly cocky on the ride back to the palace. He didn't comment on Tristan's early night, but his looks spoke volumes.

Too.

Fucking.

Loud.

As much as Tristan already wanted to be back in the palace to get away from him, he was dreading it. He wanted to see Norya, of course he did, she was his best friend, but he knew it wasn't going to be the same. She spent all of her time with him, how were things going to change? Would she feel forced to spend time with other men?

Miels sighed beside them as they neared the palace grounds. "I think we need to start a core group of men to travel for us. We all have our women now. The others are lucky. Their women are pregnant so they can stay by their sides. I can't keep leaving Etel like this."

Tristan eyed his best friend. The man was always happy, but it was clear in his eyes that being away from his wife

120

pained him. "Don't worry, mate. I'll start picking out the men I'll be leading. I don't plan on having a woman to tie me down."

Miels didn't bother acknowledging him as they traveled onto palace greens, and trotted their horses toward the stables. Not that he'd need to bring up the little barbarianette. Tristan had already promised her she'd be a part of that group.

To their shock, training beside the stables were Etel and Norya, Norya slowly backing up in order to give the smaller girl the chance to be on the offensive. It was thrilling to see them working, to see Norya training his little sister. Tristan could only imagine how hard Miels was getting seeing his wife with the sword in hand.

As the girls paused for a break, moving back toward the private training rooms, he and Miels got off their horses and deposited the animals at the stables.

When they turned for the women, Tristan dreading how Norya would act around him, they found Etel giddily tossing her sword from one hand to the other while Norya spoke with one of the stablehands. He was bigger than most of the others and great at his job.

Her smile was bright as they spoke, laugh delighted and free. She didn't look like she was being forced to do anything, definitely didn't seem like spending time with other men would be a problem for her. Matter-of-fact, she looked to be enjoying his company a little too much. More than when she'd been enjoying Eddie's company in that clearing in the forest.

Tristan couldn't let her get caught up in them. They'd only want her because they'd think she was an easy fuck. They wouldn't treat her the way she deserved to be treated. She was a goddess, a warrior, she deserved the best, and the men calling for her certainly weren't it. Were they? He certainly hadn't been so what did he know?

Tristan swallowed back the need to storm over and peel her away, forced away the need to take her, to show her that although he wasn't the man for her, their bodies were meant to spend every day together.

He watched, instead, as Miels approached them, and took his wife into his arms. "You're already too sexy, my little creature, you shouldn't be holding that sword. It'll make me mess up your pregnancy tonics."

Etel giggled, whispering something against the man's lips as he lifted her while carrying her inside.

Tristan didn't know how to feel about the small smile Norya gave him as he moved after his brother. It was soft and welcomed him home. It was exactly the kind of smile he'd expect from a friend, and that's all he wanted out of Norya.

So why did it upset him to stand there and watch as the stable hand led her to who-knew-where with his hand on her back? Why was he touching her? Why was she leaning into his touch? She'd said only a few days ago that she had feelings for him. Tristan wasn't naive enough to think they'd already gone away, but he did know she was doing as she'd promised and trying to get over him.

Tristan closed his eyes and took deep breaths. This is what he'd wanted.

"She needs to move on," he whispered to himself. "If she wants to be claimed now, she needs to find someone who wants that as well. Not all the men here will want a quick fuck, Tris. I'm sure she'll be able to tell which to give the time of day to. She knows no random fucks with palace staff are allowed. She's strong, capable, brilliant. She's gonna be fine."

When he opened his eyes, she was no longer in sight.

Tristan turned abruptly, closing his eyes once more as his fists clenched. She wasn't his woman. Just because he loved her as a best friend didn't mean he could dictate her life. He was the one who rejected her.

Tristan marched off before he did something rash and found that stablehand who had the nerve to put his hand on Nor.

He hadn't been able to get the picture out of his head, so while everyone else slept, Tristan was in the private training room boxing a sandbag. It'd been hard enough not having her company daily, not getting a proper farewell from her when going off on his trip. It had certainly been hard enough not getting a proper welcome home when he'd gotten off his horse, but the thought of her attention on another man was...

Annoying.

He was selfish, and he wanted his best friend's attention for himself.

Sweat glistened off his skin as he punched at the bag. Harder and faster, abs burning from all the work.

"You know, James doesn't like when I ogle you, but damn, who could blame me?"

Tristan whipped around to find Gemma leaning against the door that led into the palace. "What're you doing up?"

She shrugged. "Sometimes the baby's a real asshole."

"So you thought you'd come train?"

Her smile was warm, always welcoming, so very Southern. "No. I figured with the way things have been between you and Nor, you'd be up too. I tried your room first, but when you didn't answer, I figured you'd be here."

"What makes you think anything is up with Nor? She's

moving on to other men. If she wants to settle down, it's about time."

"We were with her last night. Did you hear about that? All of us girls got together to keep her company. It was actually nice for all of us to be able to rant about our men, but it was especially nice for her. We spoke of our men, and none of us brought you up. She needed the distraction... especially not knowing what you'd be doing out in those taverns."

"Just because I don't wish to claim her doesn't mean I would ever hurt her, Gem." The memory of the redhead popped up, too clear to ignore. "I was going to," he admitted. "But I thought about her the entire time, how messed up our relationship had become, and knew that I couldn't hurt her like that. It's... she wouldn't necessarily have had a way to find out but the guilt would've killed me. I can't hurt her like that."

Gemma nodded silently. She stood there for a while before moving for Tristan. She took his hand delicately into hers. "Is that why you stopped, Tris? Because you knew she has feelings for you? Or was it because another woman was touching you, and you kept thinking of Norya's touches, kept thinking about how much you only want hers, how wrong it felt to let another touch you?"

Tristan sighed. "Gem, I'm not going to claim Norya."

She ignored him. "Is it because you realized while some woman was touching you that the exact thing could be happening to Norya—another man touching her—but you realized unlike how revulsed you were, she could be enjoying the other man's touch? Did the thought of her around another male truly sink in? Or did it only start then? Did you truly realize it when you got back and saw her with Dale?"

"She's not mine. She could be with whoever she pleases."

"You know, she told me earlier how much it hurt to see you when you and Miels got back, that she has no interest in Dale but thinks that maybe if she finds another friendship here—no sex involved, still following the Posse rules—then maybe she can fall for someone else. Dale is a really good guy."

Tristan knew as much. He'd been angry earlier, but he knew Dale was a good guy. All of the stablehands were. As if working with the horses made them incapable of doing anything bad.

"She could do as she likes. She's a barbarian. When she's ready to be claimed, she can do as much."

"Kinda like how the two of you have been caught by just about everyone in this palace? Almost like you were doing it on purpose so everyone was fully aware both of you were taken? That's the claiming's 'public displays' except with a Northern twist."

"We were only fucking. The Island does that too, you know. All public fucks aren't claims."

"That's funny. I swear you two were always wandering off together, all smiles and full of conversation..."

"We were best friends—"

"Always pushing the other, always possessive of the other. I'm sure Eddie has let it be known to all the guards not to touch her because of your little show. That's very barbarian of you, Tris."

"That's not—"

"So just answer me this, and do it honestly, Tristan," she interrupted for the final time. "Can you handle the thought of her doing all of that with another male? Not just the sexual aspects, but all of it? The sex, yes, but also the teasing, the competitiveness, the protection, the camaraderie?"

"I'm not in love with her."

"So why aren't you in bed right now? Honestly."

Tristan closed his eyes to stop the tears that suddenly wanted to water. He ground his jaw to control himself, then met Gemma's beautiful eyes. "I can't sleep without her. Her fingers used to stroke my chest until I fell asleep. Or if she fell asleep first, I would stroke her back. It's been... difficult since she walked away."

Gemma kissed his knuckles, more motherly than sisterly, but comforting in a way Tristan had never experienced. "What else?"

"The forests. The boys and I used to go in for dagger throwing. Now I look at the clearings around us, and all I see is her. All I see is that time we went in together and competed on who was a better hunter—her obviously, but I would never stroke her ego so."

"And?"

"That little pout she makes when she doesn't like something. Not the way Eve or you do it to Spar and James to get your way. It's... different. Innocent. It just naturally falls on her lips—"

"Suspiciously only with you," Gemma muttered as he continued.

"When she doesn't like something, but it's never to get me to stop doing it or change anything. Things that I hadn't thought twice about before had become fun simply to see if I could get that pout from her—something from the kitchens she didn't like the taste of, a book in the library that was dustier than we'd thought once we opened it, organizing the missives—that took all day."

Gemma placed his hand on her belly, the babe kicking up a storm. No wonder she couldn't sleep. "And?"

"We would talk about... everything. Miels, Sparrow, and I have always had a strong relationship. We talked about everything. But things were easier with Nor. We let things from our past out. We talked about our days so they didn't weigh down on us. It's why we were always so happy. We let all our worries out for the other to hold on to. I talked to her in a way I never talked to anyone before."

"How's your heart right now, Tris?"

He shrugged. "Steady."

She smiled. "Normally our hearts race when we're falling for our person. That's the reason behind the butterflies. All the uncertainty, both behind whether they'd want us too, but also behind not knowing what that emotion is we're feeling. But once we're there, arrived at the destination, we tend to be steady. Safe. Secure."

Tristan shook his head, the words barely a whisper as they left him. "I'm not in love with her."

"Okay," she relented. "But be sure of that. Because you say you would never hurt her, but denying her simply because your pride says you were never meant to fall for her is hurting her more than a true denial. At least if you actually felt nothing, it would be easier for her to walk away. Right now, it's almost like dangling water in front of a dehydrated man. She, like the rest of us, sees something more in you. Either cut that tie or give in to it, just put her out of her misery."

Gemma gave a final kiss to her knuckles, then turned back for her rooms. She turned at the door with a small smirk. "Oh, by the way, none of the things you mentioned had to do with sex. Did you catch that, tough guy?"

When he was alone once more, Tristan turned back to the hanging sandbag. Instead of hitting it, he rested his arms on the thing, dropping his head as thoughts flooded him, none giving the other the proper time to process. There was just too much going on.

CHAPTER 21
NORYA

Normally Norya didn't identify as part of the Posse because she wasn't *with* anyone in the Posse. But on days she needed to be alone, she was glad the King saw her as part of his closest group. That way she could use the private training room specifically for the Posse, and no one could say a thing about it.

In the two days since Tristan had been back from his visit to the villages, she'd wanted desperately to run into his arms. When he got off his horse—something she noticed immediately from her periphery even though she tried to not pay him any attention—all she wanted was to feel his touch again. When he came near them, she swore she saw a look in his eyes, similar to the one he'd had when running Eddie off. She'd given him that warm smile because she wasn't going to put words in his mouth. If he wanted to push Dale aside and claim her, he needed to do the work.

Every time she'd seen him those two days, she'd wanted to be with him, but he never moved for her. Now, four in the morning, Norya could be in any training room and she'd be alone, but this way, no guard would find her and send gossip running. Now she could fight the imaginary man on the mats while tears slowly slid down her cheeks because she was sure —he wasn't going to fight for her, claim her. Some things simply weren't meant to be.

"You need to pay closer attention. He would've flipped you right then."

Norya jumped at the intrusion. Her heart raced at the sight of her former fuck buddy standing by the stairs, arms crossed before his chest as he watched her train. "What're you doing here?"

"I snuck into your suite so I wouldn't wake the nonas. When you weren't in bed, I figured the only other logical place would be here."

"I'm not sure this is the *only* other logical place." He knew if she really wanted to, she would break some rules and join any of the single palace men who wanted her in their beds.

His eyes darkened, and nostrils flared. "This is where I come when I have a lot on my mind."

Thankfully he wasn't acknowledging the dried tears on her cheeks. "Well, it's taken. Come back later."

"No." He moved toward her on the mats, stripping out of his shirt. "You need to let off steam. I need to let off steam. We've always been good at that."

She scoffed. "Fuck off."

As she moved to leave, he grabbed her arm and forced her into his body. "I never pegged you as scared. Pussy."

She growled, fist moving on its own as it struck into his gut.

He grunted, breathing accelerating as he smirked. "Good girl."

"Don't." She punched his stomach again. "Fucking." She

punched his chest. "Call." His face. "Me." She punched the other side of his face. "That."

He grabbed her arm before she could land another punch. "Why not? You fight instead of backing away scared. That makes me proud."

"I don't care what you are," she seethed, kicking his shin hard.

His pain gave her time to turn away, but not enough. He kicked her legs out from under her in moments, dropping her to the mats. When he landed on top of her, Norya was ready.

But so was he.

This was them. They fought. Brutally.

She punched his face, cutting his lip in the process, while his fist pummeled her stomach, winding her. When she kicked, he defended. When he elbowed, she danced away. It was never a game of cat and mouse with them. It was always cat and cat. It was only ever a matter of which cat came out with more scratches.

"You've ruined my life, Norya." He hit.

"*You've* ruined my life, asshole." She hit harder, rolling out from under him.

He kicked her. "I was content without a wife."

"I hope you remain that way because with that beat-up face, no woman will want you," she gritted as she kicked his jaw, snapping his head back.

Norya flexed her hands, readying for another attack. The asshole rejected her, and he was the angry one?

He spit some blood out as he turned dark eyes on her. "We were supposed to fuck. No romance."

"I get it," she growled. "I caught feelings. I ruined things for your perfect illusion of what life would be—"

"No fucking romance, Nor!" he yelled. "All we fucking did was romance!" He attacked her to the ground, winding her again as he forced her wrists together above her head and readied his hand around her throat. "You know I never slept with my fucks. Never teased them, competed with them, made it my life's mission to get certain reactions out of them. You've ruined me."

She didn't know why he was saying any of this, but her chest hurt with every word. She tried to fight any emotional reaction as she kicked her hips up, attempting to get him off.

It didn't work.

"You were supposed to be a fuck, Norya."

"As were you!" A tear slipped out without her permission.

He watched it, followed its trail down her cheek in the silence of the room. When it slipped onto the mat, he trailed the residue back up to her eyes. "It was so subtle. I didn't realize that would make lying to myself about our relationship easier, but it did."

"Tristan, stop—"

"You were right. I was claiming you so Eddie knew who you belonged to. So the big mouth could pass it on to everyone else. I knew it. I just wanted to keep living in the lie, thought it'd be safer there."

"I don't belong to yo—"

"I'm in love with you, Norya. Past the fucking. I'm in love with our friendship, our life. The sex is an amazing bonus, but everything else is what made me fall for you. I can't live knowing I won't get to sneak you into the kitchens to see which of us can eat more grapes or run into the dungeons to play hide and seek or compete with you on every matter."

Another tear strolled down Norya's cheek. This—everything he was saying—was all she'd wanted since she'd realized her feelings.

His hand moved from her neck to cradle her cheek, thumb swiping at the tear. "I'm sorry for letting the idea that we were still only friends blind me from realizing it as soon as you did." His mouth brushed hers. "I need you, Nor. I need to hear your laughs, listen about your day, feel your fingers running on my chest as we sleep, be inside you again. Not yet, but eventually, I need another human who is the perfect mix of us."

Norya swallowed, then fought his hand off her wrists. When he released her, still lying on top, she punched his jaw, enjoying the sound of that crack, and needing the sting of the hit.

After he spit the blood out and glared at her, she didn't give him a moment to get angry with her as she brought him down for a kiss.

Their tongues fought, needing this more than she'd thought. It was only the need for air that made them pull away.

In that time, Norya held his face between her hands and made him meet her eyes. "I'm in love with you too, Tristan. It's actually kind of an annoying feeling."

A chuckle mixed with a scoff left him. "Tell me about it."

They laughed as they both leaned in for another kiss, her hands sliding down his chest for the trouser ties as his got lost beneath her top.

CHAPTER 22
TRISTAN

Everyone was in the dining hall for dinner. The Posse had grown a great deal this year, and Tristan couldn't be happier about it. It'd meant the King needed to commission for a larger table, but he'd been happy to do so.

Beside Tristan sat Norya, who spoke to her nonas sitting beside her. Her hand drew doodles on his lap as he spoke to Sparrow and Evony about their next trip to his childhood home, and it was relaxing and distracting all at once. They were waiting for Edmund to show up to start dinner and the inevitable discussion of the plague.

Evony was pouting at her husband because the man said he wanted to wait until after she gave birth since he didn't want her riding so long when Edmund joined them. "What's she trying to convince you of now, my assassin?"

Sparrow smirked, kissing his wife's jaw as his hand caressed her belly. She was comfortable in his lap, and though she would move to her seat to eat, she didn't look in any rush to do so. "She wants a few days at the house."

"Come, boy." Edmund smiled. "We all know she'll convince you. Why even deny her?"

As the servants placed the food on the table, Sparrow bit his lip. "Her convincing is half the fun of anything, Ed."

Tristan laughed as he met Edmund's gaze. It was glittered with a 'that's my daughter you're speaking of' reprimand since he couldn't say the actual words with the servants around. It still wasn't known that Evony was his.

"Where were you?" Sparrow asked as the servants finished up.

"The third floor. I had something to check on."

Tristan's attention narrowed on the King. The third floor? What could he need to check on there? And what could he need to check on that he didn't outright tell them rather than calling it 'something?'

Tristan smirked to himself. He could be having that rendezvous with the beautiful tailor's assistant. Though the stiffness in the way he sat said that wasn't it. Maybe he'd simply been stalking her a little, watching from a distance.

"Where was he?" Norya's voice at his ear sent shivers everywhere.

"What?"

"You're looking at him like you know exactly where he was."

He turned his green orbs on her. "And what look is that?"

"Don't try to divert. Where was he?"

"Didn't you say Miels and Etel's gossiping was annoying? Should we be doing the same thing?"

She smirked. "I said it was annoying. I never said I wasn't a hypocrite."

Tristan chuckled. "I don't know where he was."

She narrowed those sexy dark eyes.

So he lowered his whisper even more to make sure they

weren't heard. "I don't. But I suspect he was wherever that tailor's assistant was."

She looked taken aback. "Atiana?"

Tristan shot his eyes around the table to make sure no one was paying attention, the King especially, then returned them to his woman. "He wants her. They want each other. But they haven't done anything about it. That's all I know."

"Why would he tell you?"

"He didn't. When the others were preoccupied with their women, I caught the two of them eyeing one another. When I said something to our dear ole king, he nearly bashed my head through the wall."

She quirked a brow. "Why does that make it sound like you said something about Atiana?"

He smirked. "I was only trying to get a reaction."

She rolled her eyes. "Don't worry. You can think she's beautiful. She is. Absolutely stunning. I'd want her too."

Tristan's brows shot up. "I'd gladly watch that."

She pushed away. "Pig."

At that moment, Edmund clapped to get everyone's attention. "Let's get the dreaded conversation out of the way— Tristan and Miels checked in on the plague. They think Ashtyn can be of use."

"We'll call a meeting with her to make sure she'd be up for it—you must remember, this isn't only outing her as a possible Master, but it's her life too. If she overexerts herself trying to do this, she could die. If she doesn't wish to risk it, we'll need to come up with other matters," Sparrow added.

"And what are those?" Nona Tereza asked.

"We'll also be getting magicians involved," Miels answered. "We're almost positive they could be of use as well."

"And lucky us," Evony added, "the one other person

outside of the Posse who seems to know about magicians is the one most likely to keep our healer safe."

"You think Gabriel will want to search for the plague's source?" Edmund asked.

"I think charming Gabriel will want nothing more than to do so. As long as he can be by the asshole healer's side," James said.

Gemma smacked him. "Don't call her that."

"What? She is an asshole. I've heard *Gabriel* call her that!"

"I know she is." Gemma smiled. "Still. Don't call her it."

James only smiled at his wife as he leaned in to kiss her cheek, his hand rubbing circles on her belly.

"Charming Gabriel could always aid in that department too," Norya added. "She could use an orgasm or seven."

They all laughed, some more than others, because of the pure accuracy of the statement.

"Then it's settled. We'll meet with Ashtyn tomorrow and start the end to this," Edmund stated. "Until then, enjoy tonight."

There was a jumble of conversation almost immediately. Tristan sat back and enjoyed it. Evony finally moved to her seat and she, Sparrow, and Edmund were in their talks of his child-hood home. Rosaelia, across from her sister, was in her own little world with her husband, Killian's full attention on the Princess. On the other end of the table, Gemma and James were in a debate with the nonas and Miels and Etel about different things that could be taught to apothecaries. And in the middle, Tristan enjoyed Norya's hand in his lap.

She leaned in close. "Once everyone has children, it's going to be a ruckus in here every night."

Tristan smiled, meeting her gaze. "I think our kids will be the loudest."

"Please tell me you're not going to be another Miels?"

He laughed. "No, darling. I am definitely not ready for kids yet. But, I'm just stating the fact—ours will be the loudest."

She shook her head. "Competitive, competitive man."

He bit his lip. "I'm sorry. You misunderstood. They're gonna get the competitive urge from you. They'll get their charms from me."

"They'll certainly be cheaters because of you."

Tristan remembered every time he'd sabotaged something they were competing in in order to win. He only winked in response, then turned to his plate and joined Evony's side of her argument just for fun.

EPILOGUE

NORYA

Sael's life must've been miserable on the Island if her cheeks were always this red. Norya never blushed but she couldn't help doing so now. It was infuriating.

She was in a dress far too short to be viewed by anyone but a significant other, and standing in front of the mirror in the second bedroom of Tristan's—now their—suite. She shared his room, but for this surprise, she wanted to make sure he wouldn't walk in on her.

He wasn't supposed to be back for another few minutes, giving Norya the time to build her confidence.

When she'd gone to Atiana for this dress, she'd blushed which had already been an anomaly for her. When she'd tried the finished product on in front of the tailor, her cheeks had pinked some more. Now, in the safety of her suite, her cheeks reddened looking at herself in the mirror.

She looked sexy, that was a given. The dress was a dark green silk that matched Tristan's eyes and barely covered her pussy with how short it was. The silk made the definition of her peaked nipples obvious and wrapped beautifully around her ass.

She had her hair down because Tristan loved it like that and a little bit of berry stained on her lips to contrast the dress.

As she turned before the mirror, the blush slowly evaporated and Norya's confidence boosted because, damn, did Atiana know how to make her look amazing.

Then she heard the door open and Tristan's voice call out. "Nor, darling. What's going on?"

Norya had copied what Tristan had done a couple weeks ago and pushed the furniture aside to leave a dance floor in the middle of the common area and set up the music box to play. Except she'd gone to Evony for her very own music box. Norya had also blushed crimson talking to the Magician about that request. Not because it insinuated the type of night she and Tristan would be having but because of how romantic it was. She wasn't used to this effort of romance.

"Sit down. I'll be right out," she called out, then waited a moment for Tristan to make his way to the couch.

When Norya stepped out of the room, Tristan's eyes widened, his jaw dropped, and his hips moved to make the space his cock was confined in more comfortable. "Wow."

She fought the blush at how girly she felt and played with the edges of the dress as she gave a little spin. "Do you like it?"

"Oh, fuck, I love it." His tongue struck out to lick his lips, eyes glued to her barely covered skin. "Are we dancing?"

"I am."

His gaze popped up, meeting hers. "What?"

"I'm dancing. You sit back, relax, and enjoy the show."

"You're going to dance for me?"

She bit her bottom lip as she nodded, devious delight in her eyes.

His arms flew up to rest on the head of the couch as he

relaxed back. "Oh, darling, I don't know what I did to deserve this but please, perform."

Perform. The word made her nervous because she wasn't a dancer yet she'd put it in her mind that she would be giving her man a show and that's what she'd do.

Gemma and Evony had helped her with this part—how in the world to dance for a man and make it sexy. They'd demonstrated and showed her the different things she could do as the other girls sat around as onlookers. It had been a mortifying moment, but watching two pregnant women teach her the allure of a sexy dance had made up for it. To give those two their credit—they knew how to lighten the mood when need be.

Not to mention, the attention the other women had given gave away that they were taking internal notes. They may have enjoyed watching her make a fool out of herself learning the moves in front of them, but Norya knew all of them would be trying them when they were in the comfort of privacy.

Norya smirked in order to hide her nerves and turned her back to him in order to wait for the beat she wanted to start on. As the music played and she waited, her fingers ran along her bare thighs, teasing the spy behind her.

"If I find out you did this for other men, Norya, I'm going to burn the Island down."

Her head fell back as she laughed, not expecting to hear that. She tilted her head to the side to catch his eyes. "This is my first time, spy. Behave."

Before he could respond, she started.

She dipped and spun for him, traced her leg with a foot and ran her hands up her body, slowing at her breasts before plunging into her hair. She moved to show off her assets, then slowly dropped to the floor to crawl to him.

He smirked as her hands crawled up his legs and played at

his thighs as she slowly rose before him and bent so her breasts were hanging in his view, swaying with the music.

He had them in handfuls in moments, kneading at the plumpness and tweaking her nipples.

She tsked as she plied his hands away. "No touching."

He growled but his hands moved back to the backs of the couch. "Sorry, darling."

She laughed as she turned between his legs, giving him another view of how perfectly the silk hugged her ass, then slowly bent over with the music. And because of the shortness of her dress, as she bent, the fabric slipped off her ass and bundled at her waist, giving him a clear view of her ass and pussy.

She twitched at the feel of something against her, then moaned when she felt his tongue slip through her folds.

She wanted to stay like that and let him enjoy his feast but forced herself to turn instead until she was face to face with the man whose hands were still biting into the couch. "No tasting either."

"You're not playing fair, Nor."

"You never play fair, Tris."

He growled as his head dipped back and he closed his eyes. "Fuck."

Her giggles continued as she turned back around and swayed her hips to the music, hands in her hair as she slowly dipped lower until she was sitting in his lap. Her hips continued to sway to the music, the feel of his cock twitching to get inside her boosting her confidence as she dipped low again.

She remained in his lap as she traced his legs down until she was playing at his ankles, pulling on his shoes as if telling him to kick them off.

He groaned, and she knew it was because her dress had

slipped up again and he was staring at her rounded ass on his trouser-covered cock. But he was still of right mind enough to kick his shoes off. Norya took care of his socks before rising and turning to face him.

She was surprised to see his shirt flying to the other end of the room and his hands at the ties of his trousers. "What're you doing?"

"You're sitting on my cock, Nor."

Her brows furrowed in mock assault. "And who said you were in charge tonight?"

"Nor, please!" The trousers went flying too.

He was naked on the couch, cock large and demanding as it lay against his stomach. She was so wet at the sight, her slickness was sliding down the inside of her legs.

She laughed as she swayed her hips, and straddled him. "Okay. But only because you're asking so nicely."

She impaled herself, and they both moaned. His hands took handfuls of her ass as he sucked on her neck, and Norya was in the heavens.

Tristan kept one hand on her ass to keep her moving, but the other cradled her face then, forcing her to meet his gaze. "I don't know how I got so lucky with you, but I'm thankful to the universe for it. And to Atiana for this dress."

Norya's smile was wide. "I love you, Tris."

"Fuck, baby, I love you more," he groaned as her pussy tightened around his cock.

with the

Winds

catching

Sunlight

catchers novel 3

NELLY ALIKYAN

WITH THE WINDS CATCHING SUNLIGHT

GABRIEL

The corridors were alive with servants running about to get the day's work done. Gabriel smiled as he passed two who were on the older side, then chucked to himself as one blushed and twiddled her thumbs. He knew some of the servants thought he was cute, and he hoped they thought him a nice guy as well. He wanted to be remembered as good, not handsome or powerful. Just plain good.

Papa Iskan, the Southern man who had come to the North in search of Evony, the Master Magician and newfound second heir to the Northern crown, always said he was as good a man as anyone could ask for. Papa Iskan wasn't shy about stating his opinion on matters, so Gabriel was especially comforted hearing it from him.

And though all that mattered to him, in reality, the only opinion he truly cared for was Ashtyn's. At the end of the day, if all else was happy with him and Ashtyn wasn't, none of it mattered. It was dangerous the amount of control that one woman had over him.

It was especially dangerous since Ashtyn did everything in

her power to act as if she wasn't affected by whatever was growing between them. Part of Gabriel figured he should give up, but an even bigger—and very nagging—part of him new that he couldn't do so. Nothing mattered to him as much as she did.

And everyone knew it.

Maybe while he was at the tailors, he could get her a gift. He knew how infatuated she'd become with many of the gowns Atiana made.

He was on his way over there anyway since Princess Rosaelia—who insisted Gabriel call her Rosaelia or the much less formal Ro—instructed him to do so in order to received a surprise, so it wouldn't hurt to look. Gabriel wasn't sure what to expect when he arrived to the suite, but he hoped Princess Rosaelia wasn't trying to set something up between him and any other member at the palace. It had happened a couple of times in the past where someone tried to set him up with a beautiful woman, but he'd never felt inclined to be with any of them.

Gabriel turned the corner to the tailors suite which was a large space with multiple areas for all the tailors to work when they weren't working in their private suites. It was oddly quiet at the moment. "Atiana, excuse me, but the Princess asked me to—"

Gabriel's mouth ran dry.

Standing before him on a slight pedestal in the most beautiful gown Gabriel had ever seen was Ashtyn. His healer.

Her gaze met his in the mirror. "What're you doing here?"

He cleared his throat. "The Princess told me there was something for me here. With Atiana." He tried to meet Atiana's gaze for longer than a glance, but he couldn't do so. Ashtyn as too hypnotizing.

Atiana's laugh was such a stark contract to Ashtyn's grimace.

"I'm sorry, Gabriel. I do not have anything for you. Do you think the Princess was trying to be cheeky? Out healer here is my only appointment of the day."

Gabriel's eyes shined as he took his time trailing down Ashtyn's curves in that dress. "She's the best surprise of my life."

Atiana's own grin was wicked. "Yes. She fills the dress perfectly, doesn't she. I cannot imagine a better woman for it."

"She's incomparable, At. There is no better woman."

"She's right here!" Ashtyn barked as her cheeks began to heat.

Gabriel's gaze shot back up to meet hers through the mirror. "And do you not think yourself incomparable in that dress? You're a beauty."

"You need to stop," she seethed through grit teeth.

Atiana giggled, pinning the final part of Ashtyn's dress. "Oh, stop it, Ashtyn. You know you like his attentions the way all the other women do."

Ashtyn's orbs darkened, then she grumbled, "I'm taking this off now."

Gabriel was stuck watching her hop off the pedestal and move for the back where she could get changed. Her hips swayed the entire way, and it took everything within Gabriel not to follow after her.

When she disappeared, and he knew she was stripping naked, Gabriel lost the inner battle, close to moving for her, when Atiana cleared herr throat and brought him back to the present.

"You look like you've seen better days, Gabriel," she joked as she eyed his clothes. They were stained from all the time he spent in the stables, and there was a rip from where Bella, one of the horses, tried to get treats from his trousers.

He chuckled. "I'm slowly running out. Eventually I'll have to start working naked."

A barely hidden choke came from the back telling him that Ashtyn as intently listening in. She always was, even when she pretended she couldn't care less.

"Oh, I was going to offer you new clothes in exchange for riding lessons, but I don't think I can deprive the entire palace from such views."

Gabriel smirked. "Don't be a tease, At. Lessons for clothes would be an easy trade, and I can use them dearly."

Atiana smiled. "It is quite a bit colder now that it is winter, so it may not be the best time to take lessons, but I'm not sure I want to wait any longer."

"No waiting needed," Gabriel insisted. "I'll call for you when the weather permits it. It is not always so back in the autumns and winters."

Atiana was smiling when Ashtyn walked out with a frown about her stunning features.

"Why so glum, beautiful?"

"Don't call me that." She wouldn't meet his gaze.

"Is it because you have to remove the gown?" Atiana joked. "Don't worry. It'll be finished soon, and you can wear it as often as you'd like."

"Great." Ashtyn gave her a smile that wasn't convincing in the slightest, then turned for the door. "I need to get back now."

Gabriel allowed the healer to pass him and took a large inhalation of her scent. When his gaze met Atiana's, hereat the teasing there. "Shut up," he muttered, then turned for his girl.

"What do you want?" Ashtyn barked when he caught up with her.

"To walk you."

"I think I am going to walk to the edge of the Southern Lands. Truly get away from you."

Gabriel laughed. "I can saddle horses to make the trip easier. Or one if you'd like to share." He wiggled his eyebrows which seemed to deepen that frown on her face, but made his smile wider.

"I'd rather walk." She sped up.

"Then I'll walk to the South with you. To the edge of the lands. Into the water if you'd like."

She didn't turn for him or say anything more, but her ears pinked. They only diid that when she was forcing herself not to smile. It'd taken him the year of watching her intently to learn as much as he could about her, and that much he was very aware of.

He wanted to take her hand, place his hand at the small of her back or the nape of her neck, have her hold him the way Evony did Sparrow, but he knew none of that would be happening. At least not yet.

Soon though, soon. That's what he'd been telling himself all year.

Continue the story in
With the Winds Catching Sunlight...

DON'T FORGET TO REVIEW!

Thank you so much for finishing your read! Don't forget to leave a review or rating on all platforms as it helps me as an author more than you can ever imagine!

Amazon and Goodreads ratings help the most but feel free to talk about it everywhere else too—including social medias, blogs, Youtube reviews, and most importantly—word of mouth, and more.

FOLLOW NELLY'S SOCIAL MEDIA

Follow Nelly's social media to get the scoop as it's happening!

- tiktok.com/authornellyalikyan
- instagram.com/authornellyalikyan
- youtube.com/NellyAlikyan
- amazon.com/author/nellyalikyan
- goodreads.com/nellyalikyan
- facebook.com/authornellyalikyan
- pinterest.com/insinpublishing

JOIN NELLY'S NEWSLETTER.

Sign up for Nelly Alikyan's newsletter to be the first to know about new releases and cover reveals, receive exclusive content —like a special scene or two—and be up to date about any other exciting news, i.e. events, signed copies, etc.

www.nellyalikyan.com

ACKNOWLEDGMENTS

To my steamy book lovers.

This one came after I started writing Ice and I realize that Norya was a character unlike any I'd written before. Sure I'd written about capable and strong women, but she was other-worldly because of the life she'd lived. And most unlike all of my girls before, she had experience... *cough, cough* you know what I mean. She's my girl who's most like my boys and a fun new route to try out.

It was also super fun learning about Tristan's full personality in writing this because he really presented himself to me in this like I was now a comfortable member of the Posse and he felt safe to do so now. I hope you all saw this as a final acceptance into the Posse as well now that even Tristan has opened up to you!

This one wasn't as steamy because I wanted to look at their relationship more than their sex since they'd started their relationship with sex, but I hope you enjoyed the ones you got. And for my steamy lovers, I know that first one was a jolt of energy!

Thank you to all of my readers for continuing on with this series.

Thank you to my family who continue to support my dreams.

Thank you to me for following my delusions!

MEET THE AUTHOR

Nelly Alikyan is a girl from the Los Angeles Valley who's constantly on the move—from Boston to London to wherever she chooses next. She's the only reader in her family—not her only cause as the black sheep—and has dreamt of being a writer for as long as she can remember.

For more books and updates:
www.nellyalikyan.com